THOSE WHO SERVE

THOSE WHO SERVE

by

A. F. BARTON

A TROJAN PAPERBACK

Published by Trojan Publications – London

Printed in Great Britain

Introduction

THOSE WHO SERVE

by

A. F. Barton

Germany had entered the war with a definite advantage over Britain. The enemy U-Boats had been taken to their strategic points before the outbreak of war and were ready to sink British shipping on sight from the moment war was declared.

Our own submarines were not idle during that period however, and this is the story of a small handful of men who went down to the sea in the little ships, alone, unprotected like the great sea convoys. Their constant enemies were the elements, the marauding Luftwaffe and the surface forces of the German Navy.

In spite of these adversities however, they came through the war with flying colours as this action packed story will show. A tremendous saga of heroism and endurance as the submarines move inexorably towards the glorious fulfilment of their purpose.

I

Dusk Patrol

A SUBMARINE is, perhaps, one of the most graceful vessels there is, all sleekness and efficient strength. Not a single inch of superfluous space on board. On the surface, she glides with a strangely irresistible force, pushing aside the waves with her bow, thrust forward by the swirling, bubbling grip of her screws.

When submerged, there is little visible but the thin, triangular wake, a rippling motion spreading out from the periscope, as the seeing eye probes the choppy horizon, always on the lookout for enemy shipping, ready to strike with a hissing of compressed air from the torpedo tubes as the slender shape of the torpedo speeds on its way towards an unsuspecting target.

The submarine *Tamaranth* moved out slowly after slipping her moorings. A low, black shape well down in the water, almost a larger version of the torpedoes she carried in her tubes, ready for any emergency.

It was now almost eight months after the outbreak of

war, the beginning of April, 1940.   And during that fate-
ful period, several thousand tons of British shipping had
been sunk by the actions of the German U-boats.   Now,
it was our chance to turn the tables to a certain extent,
to avenge some of these losses at least.

We headed out into the teeth of a strong north-westerly
wind that whipped the surface of the sea into choppy waves
that ran white across our bows.   Darkness was closing
down on us.   There would be a moon, but whether the
clouds would break sufficiently for it to show through
appreciably, was a different matter.

The Commander, Lieutenant-Commander Bill Richards
was on the bridge as usual, heavy binoculars slung casually
round his neck, his body well muffled up against the biting
wind and the salt spray which tossed continually over the
bow.

Visibility was reduced to a little under a quarter of a
mile and even with the binoculars, it was difficult to pick
out any of the details of the shoreline behind us, falling
away slowly into the white October mist.

" Wonder when we'll see that again, sir."   I jerked my
thumb idly in the direction of the land.

" Isn't it a little early to start thinking about that,
Lieutenant ? " asked Richards.

I nodded slowly.   " Yes, sir, I suppose it is."

The Commander pulled his cap further down on his head
as the wind threatened to hurl it off.   " You know, I've
been in these tin fish for nearly seven years now, but this
will be the first operational cruise against an enemy we
know is going to hit back at us if he ever gets the opportunity."

" At least we've got our chance to do some damage,

sir. These bloody U-boats have been getting it all their
own way too long. It's about time we had a crack at
things ourselves."

"You'll get your chance before you're much older."
Richards cleared his throat and gave a tight grin. His
bluff features were almost completely hidden in the shadow
of his cap. "There's only one thing I'm not too pleased
about."

"Oh, what's that, sir ?"

"It'll be full moon to-night, unless I miss my guess.
That means the enemy will have every chance to spot us
if we ever get within torpedo range. Not only that, but
it throws so many damned trickly shadows that it's impossible to tell whether you've got anything in your sights or
not."

As the darkness deepened, we ran submerged. It was
unlikely that the enemy would have air patrols out at night
in that particular area, but there was no point in taking
unnecessary chances; and the moonlight would help them
considerably if they were around.

By dawn, we were off the Orkneys. Now, the sea was
really up. Great troughs of it, funnelled by the wind,
ripped into a confused area of white-capped waves by the
cross-currents. In all, we found it disconcerting.

We surfaced after the Commander had taken his usual
quick look around the horizon through the periscope.
It was more instinctive than necessary. There would be
few enemy ships approaching the British Isles as closely
as that, but there was always the possibility of running
into a U-boat.

On all sides, the sea stretched away in a grey plain,
bounded by the grim, forbidding cliffs of the Orkneys a

little distance off the starboard bow. Behind us, the submarine laid a vanishing furrow of white into the waves. Above us, the sun shone synthetically with little heat. A storm was advancing from almost directly ahead, long black streamers and curtains dropping down to the horizon.

It was the visible warning of the weather we had been expecting to hit us before the trip was finished. It now looked as though we were about to experience it before the trip was half over. The submarine was bucking like a wild thing now, her bow drinking deep of the water. Now and then, great waves would explode over the bows and drench everybody on the bridge.

A sweeping lather of salt spray lashed over us as we made our way forward, Richards cursing our luck as he made his way to the bridge with practiced steps.

The lookouts were already in position, although they would probably not be required until we entered enemy waters. Tugging his cap down against the plucking, slapping fingers of the wind, the Commander yelled.

" Seen anything yet ? "

The lookouts yelled something in return, but their words were snatched from their lips by the wind and it was difficult to make them out. They were shaking their heads however, and the import behind their reports was obvious.

The sea grew rougher as the morning progressed, the sky lowering. The storm advanced towards us, climbing into the grey dome of the sky, blotting out the wintry light of the sun. Long fingers of rain reached down into the sea. The wind freshened even further.

The stark, bleak outline of the Orkneys fell away behind us as we proceeded across the North Sea towards the German shipping lanes. Soon, they were gone altogether, vanishing into the mist and the greyness of rain.

Visibility dropped even further after that. By mid-day, it had fallen to less than a couple of hundred yards and was still worsening as the *Tamaranth* became enveloped in squally rain showers.

The crew were all in top spirits. It was the beginning of their first operational mission, the chance to have a crack at the enemy. The disappointments and the frustrations which would inevitably follow had not yet had time to make themselves felt.

The Lieutenant-Commander kept every man on his toes from the very beginning. There was to be no over-assurance, no lapse into a false sense of security and over-confidence. That was dangerous in any branch of the Navy, but doubly so in the submarines.

Throughout the afternoon, we ran before the storm, pushing steadily eastwards, remaining submerged most of the time, for we were gradually approaching enemy waters and the chances of encountering enemy surface forces or planes was increasing with every hour.

There was apparently no shipping in the main lanes of the North Sea. For several hours, we saw nothing. The storm blew itself out during the latter half of the afternoon and we surfaced for a little while, keeping a sharp lookout. There was nothing.

Once we caught a glimpse of a smudge of smoke on the horizon, but it was moving away from us far swifter than we would be able to travel and reluctantly, we watched it vanish over the edge of the sea, dropping gradually out of sight.

" Hell and Damnation," muttered Richards as he

watched it go. "Our first chance, and we have to be so far away when we spot it that we can't manoeuvre into an attacking position. Why the hell couldn't it have been a tanker loaded to the beams so that she was lying so deep in the water she could hardly move?"

"You wouldn't want to pick off a sitting duck for your first target, would you sir?" asked Conway, the Chief Engineer.

Conway was a small, taciturn man, placid enough under ordinary circumstances, but capable of flying into fearful rages when crossed, especially about his beloved engines.

"If it's a bloody Jerry, I'll pick it off no matter what kind of a target he makes," roared Richards.

Ten minutes later, he gave the order. "Diving Stations!"

The hatch of the conning tower was slammed shut and clipped. Slowly, we dived, levelling out at depth. The Shetlands were just visible off the port bow as we submerged.

"Get the crew together, Lieutenant. I want them all assembled in the fo'c'sle," said the Commander sharply. "It's about time they knew the details of our mission."

The crew assembled silently in the tiny, narrow torpedo compartment, lit by naked, wire-caged bulbs that glowed whitely in the dimness, picking out the faces of the men. There was insufficient space for them to be fallen-in.

In the cramped quarters, between the folding bunks of the ratings, they squeezed themselves together, some squatting on the yielding bunks, others pushed as far back as the breech-blocks of the torpedo tubes.

Most of them waited tensely. Others, in an attitude of forced casualness, looked up in mild surprise as the Commander entered. I mustered them quickly and reported to the Lieutenant-Commander.

Richards came in and eyed each of the men in turn. The familiar faces that had been with us for the best part of a year. Ridsey, leading telegraphist, Murray, Davies and Williams. Lander, the torpedo-gunner; standing beside Gardiner the mate.

"Seems the Germans are sending several troop transports along the Norwegian coast. Whether they'll land or not, we don't know. But our orders are to sink as much of the enemy shipping as possible. We'll have to be careful though. There's likely to be a concentration of our own shipping there.

"From now on, all lookouts will keep their eyes open. I want to know immediately a ship is sighted. If we're lucky we should be able to do some damage this trip. At least, I sincerely hope so."

Someone whistled silently through their teeth. There was the usual nervous shuffling of feet, followed by prolonged coughing. There was urgency in their faces. At last, they knew their objective.

Two days later, we had reached a point some ten miles out from Bergen. The , fiordic coast of Norway was still out of sight, below the lip of the horizon. The weather had brightened considerably and visibility had increased to two or three miles.

At last, we had our first encounter with an enemy ship. We had surfaced in the calm of evening dusk, discontented a little with the mononotous lack of incident save for the usual false alarms and the sighting of a couple of enemy aircraft. These, however, did not see us and flew off towards the south-east, vanishing into the clouds.

Twenty minutes or so after surfacing, smoke was sighted to the south-east. Through the binoculars, Richards eyed it critically. It might be one of our own ships, even perhaps, a neutral, although this was hardly likely.

" Can you make it out, sir ? " I asked tensely.

" Afraid not. Too far away at the moment." Richards lowered his glasses and stood for a moment, rubbing his eyes, where the rimmed lenses had made deep red marks in the skin. " She's heading in this direction at the moment, but I'm expecting her to turn away towards the coast if she's an enemy ship."

I screwed the binoculars into my eyes, bracing myself as the submarine rolled slightly. It was easy to pick out the pillar of smoke on the horizon, but difficult to pick out any details of the ship beneath it.

Ten minutes later, it was possible to see that she was, indeed, turned away slightly towards the invisible coast of Norway. Our belief that she was a German ship was thereby increased. The strange part of it all, was the fact that she was travelling alone, unescorted.

I voiced my doubts to the Commander, who merely shrugged his broad shoulders.

" Maybe they don't think we'll dare come in so close to the coast," he remarked. " If that's what they're thinking, they've another opinion coming. We'll make a submerged attack."

The wind had dropped considerably during the past two days and the sea was quite calm. Through the growing darkness of dusk, it was just possible to keep the distant ship in sight as we stumbled back to the conning tower, clambered down into the interior, heard the hatch slam shut with a dull, metallic clatter a second before Richards gave the order to dive.

Now that the storm had abated, it was relatively easy to keep the *Tamaranth* on an even keel when submerged. We moved closer, Richards at the periscope, his eye glued to the lens.

" Port twenty," he ordered tersely. " Bring her round."

No perceptible change, but the new course must have been taken up, for a couple of minutes later, he gave a sigh of satisfaction and said: " That's good. Hold her steady at that."

The *Tamaranth* thrust on into the darkening night, almost due east, the mechanically enhanced vision of the periscope enabling the Commander to keep the distant ship in sight.

" We're in luck this time," he said finally, taking his face away from the periscope. " She's a German vessel, all right. A big one too, by the look of her, although it's getting darker with every minute."

He moved aside and motioned me forward, pointing towards the eyepiece. I went forward and peered through the eyepiece turning the periscope slowly from side to side, waiting until my eyes had become adapted to the darkness outside before attempting to see anything.

It was desperately important to keep the eye moving, never gazing at any one particular spot for any length of time. That would be fatal.

Finally, I was able to make out the distinctive shape of the enemy ship. She was travelling dark, with no lights showing and zig-zagging slightly, not too much to indicate that she knew of our presence, but sufficiently to give herself away as an enemy with a guilty conscience.

I stepped back and the Commander resumed his place. He evidently spotted the ship immediately for his back seemed to stiffen unconsciously. Then he roared: " Battle stations ! Stand by one and three tubes."

The control room seemed to be crowded all at once. Men seemed to be everywhere. I took a quick look round, saw that everyone was at his battle station, then reported to the Commander.

" All correct, sir."

" Good. Then here's hoping our luck holds, eh ? "

II

Torpedoes Running !

A FEW seconds elapsed. Completely silent, we crept forward, towards a still unsuspecting target. At last we were close enough to make out the outline and general details. It was a troop carrier of some eight or nine thousand tons, lying heavily in the water.

Richards was silent for a long moment after it had been identified as an enemy. There was a worried expression on his rugged features. He rubbed his chin thoughtfully.

I knew what he was thinking. The same thought had struck me a few moments earlier. No escort ! Even for the Germans, that was well—ungehört. No Captain in his right mind would travel alone in these waters.

Was it a trap ? Was this ship the bait, temptingly placed to catch any British submarine stupid enough to attempt to attack ? Richards leaned forward and swept the entire horizon. He was looking for any other vessels, lurking in the vicinity, waiting to pounce once we gave ourselves away. The track of a torpedo would be spotted immediately if there were any lookouts posted on the troop-ship. Evasive action, if carried out promptly would be possible, and the torpedo could run past the target and explode harmlessly some distance away. And that would be the signal for the others to converge on our position.

Richards seemed to be deliberating the problem within himself. Finally, biting his lower lip, he glanced across at me.

"Think it could be a trap, Lieutenant?" he asked tautly.

I shook my head. "I don't see how it can be. There's nothing else in sight. We're still five miles or so from the coast and we've seen nothing of enemy aircraft."

"There may be a U-boat prowling around, waiting for us to give ourselves away."

"I think that's a chance we'll have to take, sir. We should be able to put a torpedo into her and still get away without too much trouble."

"Maybe you're right, Lieutenant. We'll chance it anyway. No sense in coming all this way if we don't attack."

Carefully, we snaked our way towards the target. Her speed was estimated at fifteen knots. Certainly not much more. Range five hundred yards.

We had a free field of operation. Nothing to hinder us. No other ship to overlap and get in the way. It certainly looked as though our first victim was going to be easy meat.

Slowly, we reduced speed to match that of the troop carrier. At last, we were on the hunt. Our quarry was in sight and drawing steadily closer. The wireless operator reported that no signals had been given out by the enemy vessel. She was obviously travelling completely closed up.

Three hundred yards. Almost within accurate torpedo range. Slowly, the tension mounted. There was absolute silence on board the *Tamaranth*. Men exchanged significant glances. Everyone stood by, ready for the order to fire.

" Tubes one and three to the ready." The order is given.

" Tubes ready, sir ! "

The Commander took aim. I could visualise what was happening. The intense sensation of elation as the target glides steadily into the field of view, creeping towards the crosswires. Slowly, gently. The forepart of the troop ship will be almost touching and still no sign from the enemy that he even guessed at our presence there, lying within a couple of hundred yards, the torpedoes ready to run at a moment's notice.

" Fire ! " Richards snapped the word from the corner of his mouth without taking his eyes from the eyepiece. The low, sibilant hiss of air pressure was just audible, followed by the metallic click of the tube levers.

The *Tamaranth* seemed to jerk backwards a little at the recoil, bouncing slightly at the shock of the discharge.

There was a moment's pause, then: " Torpedoes running, sir ! "

" Good. Tubes two and four load ! "

The order was carried out promptly. There was just the chance that the other torpedoes would run awry, miss their target through some unknown chance and it was as well to be ready to fire again. There might never be a second chance if the remaining tubes were unloaded.

During the seconds that followed, the sensation of tense expectancy rose sharply. Everybody seemed to be listening with bated breath, waiting for the explosion which would announce a hit, or the prolonged silence which would tell us that the torpedoes had gone awry.

There were so many things that could happen. No two torpedoes are alike in all respects. They each have their own individual characteristics. Sometimes, the best of torpedoes, fired correctly from less than a hundred yards, missed and carried on past the target.

At others, a patched up torpedo, fired from a faulty tube, which by rights should miss whatever the range, scores a direct hit. There is no way of telling what a torpedo is going to do once it had been fired. All one can do, is wait and see.

Richards seemed to be staring sightlessly into the night darkness, watching and waiting as breathlessly as the rest of us. After what seemed an eternity, but what in reality could only have been seconds, the roar of the explosion beat against the *Tamaranth* like a blow from some gigantic, invisible fist.

Richards sucked in his breath through his teeth. When he pulled his face away from the eyepiece, it was aglow with elation.

" Take a look at that, Lieutenant," he exclaimed joyously. " I've waited months to see a sight like that. And now, at last, it's happened."

I peered through the eyepiece. No need to waste time staring around the horizon, this time. There, right in the centre of the crosswires, slowly drifting out of them, was the German troop carrier, half hidden behind a rising pall of water, thrown up by the force of the explosion.

Already, fire was beginning to flicker along her sides, climbing up towards the masts. Smoke was pouring from her upper deck, obscuring the view so that it was difficult to make out details. There seemed to be feverish activity on board.

Boats were being lowered and men were scrambling into them and rowing away from the stricken ship.

" She's going down, all right," I said tensely. " There's no doubt about that. They're abandoning ship."

" Excellent." Richards seemed almost beside himself. " That's one troop ship that won't reach their forces in Norway." He sobered instantly. " Perhaps after that, we ought to make ourselves scarce. He may have friends hanging around in the vicinity and I don't want to have a couple of destroyers on our necks."

There was no time for reflection. We had sunk our first victim and a good one at that. Nine thousand tons was the Commander's estimate with perhaps a thousand men on board. It was impossible to tell how many would eventually make it to land. There were five miles or so to cross before they reached the Norwegian coast and several of the men must have been killed during the explosion.

Twenty minutes later, there was no sign of the ship.

She seemed to have disappeared entirely. With her reduced speed, it was impossible that she should still be afloat and making for port. As no further vessels made their appearance, we searched the area for half an hour, but found nothing apart from a little wreckage strewn over the surface of the sea.

Steering almost due south, we submerged for a period to reload the empty tubes and make ready for any further action now that we had entered the enemy shipping lanes. Oddly enough, for the first half of the next day we spotted nothing. Once we saw smoke on the horizon, only to find on closer inspection that it was nothing more than a couple of fishing vessels.

As their nationality was in doubt and they were too small to sink anyway, we ignored them and moved cautiously down the coast of Norway.

15.50 hours and still no sign of anything. The shipping lanes seemed to be remarkably clear of shipping. Our luck seemed to be dead out.

We remained submerged for long periods during that afternoon. The sun was brilliant and we would have been easy targets from the air. Shortly before 17.00 hours, we surfaced and took a quick look around.

The sky was clear and blue with no sign of cloud and there, less than half a mile away and heading straight in our direction was an enemy destroyer. Had we been seen ? It was impossible to tell, but there was no doubting the fact that it was unhealthy to stay on the surface a moment longer than was absolutely necessary.

Richards tumbling down the narrow ladder into the

control room, found his voice in a harsh rattle of sound.
" Alarm ! Battle stations ! "

A moment later. " Hatch closed ! Flood ! "

We went down rapidly, levelling out below periscope
depth. Men moved swiftly, cursing beneath their breath.
Breathlessly, we waited for the depth charges to fall around
us. Tensely, we listened for the explosions which would
tell us that we had been seen.

As was normal in circumstances such as this, there was
absolute silence throughout the boat. Not a whisper.
We strained our ears to pick out the sound of propellers
above us, but could hear nothing.

Ten minutes crept by; and then another ten. Still no
sound to break the silence.

" Think he's still there ? " whispered Richards finally,
putting his lips close to my ear. " Funny we can't hear
anything. You'd think he'd have dropped depth charges
by now if he knew we were here."

" Maybe he's not sure," I whispered back. " Perhaps
he's waiting to pick us up, listening out for us."

Gently, we crept up to periscope depth. Richards took
a quick look, swinging the periscope round to cover the
full circle of seeable view. I tried to visualise what he was
seeing from the expression on his face, but it told me
nothing. He was giving nothing away.

Finally, he looked across at me, puzzled. " Can't see
anything of him," he said in a bewildered tone. " He
seems to have disappeared."

" Should we surface, sir ? " I asked.

" It could be risky. Still, I suppose we can chance it.

There's nothing showing in the periscope."

We surfaced, the water pouring off the steel sides of the submarine in a shower of foaming spray. There was nothing to be seen of the German destroyer. The sea around us was completely empty.

"That's funny," muttered Richards. He raised his binoculars then thought better of the action and allowed them to fall around his neck again. "I wonder where the devil that destroyer got to. No sign of her now."

He continued to mutter curses under his breath as we continued on our way. Perhaps, I thought, it was lucky we had dived when we had. An encounter with a destroyer was a totally different proposition to that with a loaded troop carrier.

My reverie was broken by a sudden shout from the starboard lookout. He was pointing excitedly in the direction of the enemy coast. At first, I could see nothing, then dimly, above the roar of the wind, I could make out what he was shouting.

"Enemy aircraft approaching. I think they've spotted us."

Within seconds, Richards had herded us inside the conning tower and was clambering down himself. For the second time within a few hours, we were forced to crash dive. The alarm signal screamed through the *Tamaranth*.

For a long moment, I had the crazy impression that the boat was not going to dive, that she was no longer answering her controls. It was a maddening, frightening experience.

At any moment, the enemy aircraft would be dropping its bomb load and then there would be no time for us to escape. For what seemed an eternity, the *Tamaranth* clung to the surface like a frightened child, afraid of the dark depths which were now her only hope.

Then, quite suddenly, she obeyed and we went down like a stone. Silently, we waited for the crash of bombs. There seemed to be little doubt in any of our minds that we had been spotted while on the surface.

"Nothing yet," said Richards. He pulled himself rigidly upright.

"Maybe he didn't see us after all," I muttered, trying to force conviction into my tone.

"That's hardly likely. We must have looked as big as a bloody battleship from up there. He couldn't help seeing us. We'll be lucky if— "

He broke off. The first of the shattering explosions sounded from almost directly overhead. It was followed a couple of seconds later by another, and yet another. The submarine rocked madly and it was virtually impossible to remain upright for any length of time.

The attack lasted the best part of a quarter of an hour. Richards did everything he could to throw off the enemy bomber. In the end, the dull muffled booming of the bombs dwindled away into silence. We waited with bated breath for a further ten minutes before coming up to periscope depth.

There was the possibility that it was a trick on the part of the enemy pilot to lure us out onto the surface again. Perhaps a signal had already been flashed out to the Naval forces that a British submarine was operating in the vicinity, and giving our position.

Unless we got out of that particular area soon, we were in for a packet of trouble. And nobody knew that better than the Commander. A touch of the hand mechanism and the periscope motor hummed faintly, sending the steel shaft sliding upwards.

" Nothing showing," muttered Richards after a moment-ary pause. " The trouble is we can't see much from here when they're in the air. We'll have to surface to be com-pletely sure."

Slowly, cautiously, we went up, breaking surface five minutes later. Richards was the first up the narrow ladder leading into the conning tower. As No. 1 I followed close behind. There was the unmistakable clatter of heels below me and the ladder started to shake slightly as some-one else began to climb.

Instrument panels glowed in the darkness of the conning tower. The helmsman was just visible as a moving shadow with only his hands and part of his features visible in the faint glow from the panels.

Outside, it was cool and dark with the moon, approach-ing its third quarter hanging low on the horizon, throwing an unbroken bridge of light across the smooth surface of the sea. The sun had set almost an hour earlier although there was still a faint red glow in the west marking the place where it had sunk below the surface of the sea.

Rapidly, Richards and I swept the sky through the binoculars. There was no sign of the enemy aircraft and few clouds in which he could be hiding, ready to deliver a sneak attack against us.

" Looks as though he's given up the idea of searching for us," said Richards with a sigh of relief. He lowered his glasses.

" Either that, or he considered that his bombs had damaged us sufficiently to put us out of commission," I replied.

I took another quick look around. The horizon was just distinguishable below a deepening pall of darkness. A long bank of cloud lay immediately above the moon, low down in the east and above it, stretching up to the zenith and far down behind us, the sky was filled with the glory of stars.

Corona Borealis, Boötes and Ursa Major climbing up in a great, wheeling movement around the Pole Star. I jerked my attention back as something far down, below the stars and the moon and the cloud caught my eye. Richards had obviously seen it too, for I heard his sudden indrawn hiss of breath between his teeth.

" Two of them. What luck. And I thought we were going to be damned lucky if we bagged one victim. This must be one of their main shipping lanes between Germany and Norway."

The twin columns of smoke, barely visible against the darkness of approaching night, were close together, almost indistinguishable as separate entities except through the magnifying eyes of the binoculars.

Whoever they were, they were obviously travelling in company and that presented complications, especially if they turned out to be a couple of the big fellows, such as cruisers or destroyers.

Richards clasped his hands together and waved them above his head. The characteristic motion was obvious. Once more our luck was in. We had a full compliment of torpedoes, having used up only a couple on the troop carrier. And if the worst came to the worst, we could always use the gun.

III

Into Battle

22.30 and we were within torpedo range of the two enemy vessels. In the moonlight, the distance was impossible to determine accurately. Such things as speed and direction are all but meaningless at full moon or thereabouts. One can only proceed by a kind of ingenious guesswork that works well sometimes and breaks down disastrously at others.

As usual, the control room was crowded as we submerged and levelled out at periscope depth. This was going to be a tricky business. The two ships were almost in line and zig-zagging about like nobody's business, making it devilishly difficult to keep them in the sights for any decent length of time.

The Lieutenant-Commander was swearing under his breath continuously, working himself up into a pitch of excitement. His lips moved in the grey shadow of his face, but no words came out.

" Have we got within range of these two ships yet, sir ? " The leading telegraphist came forward, hesitantly.

I nodded absently, my mind on other things. A moment later, Richards called me forward and motioned me to take a look through the periscope. Acting on impulse, I closed my eyes for a few seconds before attempting to pick out the targets.

As soon as I opened them, I realised it was a mistake. The moonlight, scattering into a million sparkling fragments off the waves, reflected the yellow brilliance right into the periscope, almost blinding me. I blinked several times and swore softly under my breath.

I began to see what Richards had meant when he had said that brilliant moonlight hampered everything for a submarine commander. Gradually, my eyes accustomed themselves to the vivid glare and I was able to make out the twin shapes of the two vessels.

I realised then why the other had seemed so excited. Here was a real prize if only we could get at it. A tanker, loaded to the rails with precious cargo, wallowing heavily in the seas. It was even possible to see the waves breaking in a splashing foam over her decks as she ducked deeply with every swell.

I turned the periscope slightly to take in the silhouette of the other ship. What I saw made me realise that it was not going to be such an easy job as I had hoped. The other was a destroyer. There was no mistaking the sleek lines and grim purpose of her outline.

I suppose my face must have fallen perceptibly, because quite suddenly, Richards gave a quick laugh and said grimly:

"It's much as I expected. They wouldn't allow such a precious cargo as that to go unattended, especially as they now know that there is a British submarine operating somewhere in these waters. But you never gain any worthwhile prize without having to fight for it. And the added danger gives spice to the adventure."

"Which are you going to attack first?" I asked.

Richards rubbed his stubbly chin with a gesture which was fast becoming characteristic of him when deliberating.

"The destroyer I think. The tanker can't make much headway with that load on board. But as for the destroyer, that's different. She's got a damned good turn of speed and she's the more dangerous of the two.

"I think we ought to take a chance on putting her out of action first if it's humanly possible. We'll have the advantage of surprise on our side and that should tip the scales in our favour. At least, I hope so," he added with a crooked grin on his lips.

Like a wolf tracking a herd of sheep, we followed close on the heels of the two ships. As yet, there was no sign from either of them that they even guessed at our presence in the immediate vicinity.

"Tubes two and four clear!" muttered the Commander sharply.

"Tubes clear, sir." The reply came back almost immediately.

"Tubes two and four ready."

A slight pause, then the answer. "Tubes ready, sir."

"Good." The Lieutenant-Commander whispered the word almost to himself. "Now we'll show them what we're made of. And in no uncertain manner."

There was a grim expression on his broad features as he glued his eye to the eyepiece, his hands gripping the guides. There was something of a huge dynamo about Lieutenant-Commander Richards, I decided. It was curious that I had not noticed it before.

An irrepressible driving force that seemed to spur him on, especially in these moments before we closed in for a kill.

It was not a particularly easy matter to keep the *Tamaranth* straight on course in the heavy swell which was running across the bows, but somehow it was managed. The sea was still running high, but the wind had died almost completely and there seemed to be scarcely a breath of air.

"This is going to be damnably difficult," muttered Richards, half to himself. "This bloody moonlight spoils everything. How can you expect to hit anything when it throws so many damned shadows you can scarcely tell which is the ship and which isn't ?"

We went into silent routine. Words and orders were given in whispers. In the engine room, where they were used to the noise, they used a weird sign language of their own concoction. We closed in as quickly as we dared. There was a chance that the enemy destroyer was not only alert, but listening out for us. If that were the case, we would have to slam a couple of torpedoes into her as soon as possible, then get outside the range of her guns until the explosions had had their effect.

Then, and only then, would there be time to go for the bigger prize—the tanker.

The tubes were all ready. The men were all at their

action stations, ready for the command to fire.   Richards licked his lips with a peculiarly hungry motion of his tongue.   There was tenseness written all over his posture and the whiteness of the knuckles where they tightened with nervous pressure.

" Number Two tube — ready."   A pause, then : " Number Two tube—fire ! "

The faint hiss of compressed air.   The barely perceptible shiver of the boat as the torpedo leaves its tube and begins its journey towards the sliding shape of the destroyer.

Someone begins to count off the seconds as we listen for the explosion.   Nothing.   Something must have gone wrong.   Either we had miscalculated the distance, or the speed of the destroyer.

" Tube Number four—fire ! "   The order came out in a single blue of sound, so that it was almost impossible to distinguish between one syllable and the next.

The pause of perhaps a single heartbeat and then the strange shiver.   Another torpedo was on its way.   Better luck to that one, I thought.   Vaguely, I was aware of the fact that the Commander was giving the order for the other tubes to be loaded, his voice cutting into my mind above the monotonous counting of the man with the stop watch.

God, I thought wildly.   Had that one gone awry too ? Had we missed again through some particular detail we had overlooked in the heat of the moment ? Had the moonlight played its insidious tricks again, making a couple of hundred yards suddenly expand like elastic into five hundred ?

I realised that I was holding my breath until it hurt in my lungs. Quite suddenly, I released it in an audible sigh and at the same moment, there came the distant *boom* of an explosion.

Richards, who had straightened for a brief moment, placed his eye back to the periscope, his mouth set in a thin line across the centre of his features. Then he smiled.

" Direct hit amidships," he called. " Here, Lieutenant, take a look for yourself. See what you think to that."

Excitedly, I peered through the periscope. The destroyer was almost engulfed in a rising curtain of water, but even as I watched, it settled slowly and it was possible to see the wicked glint of flames burning just above the waterline. We were quite close to her, but moving away slowly, just in case she still had some fight left in her. The tanker would be easy meat once her companion destroyer had been put out of action.

" We may as well give her another torpedo," said Richards suddenly, coming forward. " Prepare to fire tube number one ! "

" Tube number one ready for firing, sir."

We closed in again for the final blow. The motors were giving everything they had got as we drove nearer. The tension rose steeply. It ended suddenly as Richards gave the order to fire.

This time there was not as long to wait before the dull thunder of the explosion. Whether we were closer or whether we had grown a little used to success, it was difficult to tell.

" They're worried," shouted Richards. " Some of them are taking to the boats. I think she's going down."

" Thank God for that," I muttered. " I was expecting trouble from that quarter."

" We'll take the tanker now," said Richards casually. He seemed to have regained some of his composure. " She's a sitting duck." He looked across at me significantly as he said it, and there was a brief smile on his lips.

The destroyer went down in a vast, spreading whirlpool of oil-shot water. There were lifeboats pulling away from the scene and once or twice, I caught a glimpse of dark shapes that floated past the submarine, dead faces picked out by the vivid glow from the sinking destroyer.

" Port ten," ordered Richards sharply.

There was a pause, then:

" On target ! "

Tanker Destroyed !

BY now, the German tanker was taking drastic avoiding action. The knowledge that a British submarine was in the vicinity must have penetrated their minds the instant the destroyer had been struck.

"We've got them worried," muttered Richards jubilantly. "I can see them running about on deck quite plainly. Some of them are trying to lower the boats."

"You can't blame them," I remarked, watching the play of emotions over his broad features. Elation and determination all blended together as he strove to conceal his feelings from the rest of us until the mission had been carried through to a successful conclusion.

The first torpedo rose from the rough water some thirty yards from the bow of *Tamaranth* and careened across the created waves like a flat stone skimmed across the still waters of a pond.

Richards took over again, screwed up his face in consternation and swore softly under his breath.

" A high runner," he muttered. " That's just the kind of luck we needed when every second counts. Tube three—fire ! "

Again we heard the faint, keening hiss of compressed air followed by the slight shudder of recoil. Richards' face was tight and grim. In the half-light, only his tight-fisted grip on the periscope guides showed that he was not a stranger.

A moment of paralysing suspense, then the Commander's sudden expulsion of breath as the torpedo struck home. The roar of the explosion was louder than before. A thunderous, flat sound that could be distinctly heard, even at periscope depth.

" Take her up ! " roared Richards sharply. He turned to me. His face was a study. " No sense in wasting any more precious torpedoes," he said quietly. " We'll finish her off with the four-incher. Give the gun-crew a spot of practice."

Five minutes later, we had surfaced, keeping a wary eye in the direction of the burning destroyer which might still have proved troublesome.

The tanker lay off the starboard bow, blazing fiercely. Already, she had a decided list and even as we watched, there came another thunderous explosion amidships. There was no time for reflection. The coast was still clear as far as the destroyer was concerned. No sign of any danger there for the moment. Whether there was still anyone on board her, waiting to open fire as soon as we came within killing range, it was too early to tell.

" Gun-crew on deck. Prepare to fire as soon as I give the order ! "

The clatter of feet on the narrow ladder and the dull clang of the conning-tower hatch falling back were the only sounds that followed the Commander's sharp order. The first shock of the call to action had set off a nervous thrill of excitement inside me. Something that was felt by all of the other men inside the submarine. Torpedoing was all right when it was necessary to remain submerged because of attack from surface craft. But only the man at the periscope could see anything of the action.

Now it was different. The gun-crew hurried to their gun, began to handle it with trained precision. Lieutenant-Commander Richards would have no slackers on his ship. Every man had been trained, so that he knew exactly what to do when the necessity arose.

It looked as though the tanker was going straight to the bottom without any additional help from us, but Richards knew, as well as the rest of us, that there had been instances in the past when a vessel had been left in what seemed to be a sinking condition and had yet managed to make it back to port, complete with its precious cargo.

This was not going to happen in this case. We were determined about that. I wiped my face unfeelingly, as salt spray lashed over it. The sea was unusually choppy for the time of year, but in these waters one could expect anything.

Richards, with his binoculars glued to his eyes, was

staring out at the slowly sinking tanker. The four-inch gun, mounting on a section of revolving breastwork, was ready for action within minutes, the crew standing by for the Commander's order to fire, the wicked-looking barrel pointing in the direction of the tanker.

Still no fire from the listing destroyer to port.

Richards yelled to the gunner.

" Can you see the target all right from there ? "

" Target, sir ! "

Glasses up, I listened to the clattering of the men's heels on the metalwork. The submarine was wallowing like some giant porpoise in the heavy swell, making it difficult to stand steady, even when braced against the bridge. How the members of the gun-crew were managing was something of a miracle.

" All right !   Open fire ! "

There was a short pause, then the four-incher opened up with an ear-blasting bellow. There was no necessity to watch the reloading drill. This was the job for which the men had been trained. If they did not know it now, they never would.

I found myself staring through the binoculars at the long, black silhouette of the tanker, lying heavily in the water, brilliantly lit by the flames pouring from her hold. The majority of her crew had already taken to the boats and were pulling away from the stricken ship as hard as they could go.

A thin spout of white-edged water erupted into sudden being a couple of yards short of the starboard bow. It was followed by a second a moment later, almost on the waterline.

" Bloody good shooting," said Richards' quiet voice beside me. There was a throb of exultation in it which I detected immediately.

His tenseness was betrayed by the way his cheeks were hollowed, by the erectness of his bearing as he stood holding his glasses to his eyes with one hand, the other gripping the edge of the bridge. Now on target, the gun-crew had opened rapid fire, smothering the tanker with shells. Time and again, it was possible to see the shells exploding on the target, their glowing flashes seemingly feeble against the blazing inferno which had now eaten away half of the ship.

" Cease fire ! " ordered Richards suddenly. He leaned forward over the windbreak of the bridge to yell his command, shouting to be heard above the booming of the gun. Silence fell as the crew straightened and looked about them across at the scene of destruction. they had helped to wreck.

Richards ordered automatically. " That should be enough to finish her. You've had your practice lads. You've done well."

For a long moment after that, I turned my attention away from the sinking tanker and looked forward, past the ugly snout of the four-incher, towards the bow of the *Tamaranth*. It was my favourite view of the submarine. A single view which gave the entire picture of her strength and efficiency and singleness of purpose. A deadly creature of streamlined steel lying completely in my vision.

One of the most modern of all British submarines, she had a displacement of one thousand and ninety tons on the surface, increasing to fifteen hundred and seventy five tons when submerged. A slender brute of a ship, two hundred and seventy-five feet of power-packed steel.

Below the deck were housed the powerful diesel engines which gave us a surface speed of over fifteen knots. Yet even with these great engines, it was necessary to have an alternative method of propulsion when submerged. The diesels would have consumed air, which was precious and consequently, there were the electric motors which gave us the nine knots underwater speed.

A tremendous explosion caused my mind to turn over completely in my head, breaking my train of thought. God, I thought, the tanker has blown herself up. I turned my head automatically to take in every detail of the sinking ship, scarcely aware that Richards was shouting something urgently in my ear.

Only gradually, did the words penetrate. "The destroyer! They've opened fire. We can't hope to fight them off on the surface. Everybody below ! Hurry ! "

More clattering of feet, a frenzied clattering this time, and Richards caught me tightly by the arm dragging me down the ladder into the control room. There was no time to be lost. That last salvo of shells from the destroyer had barely missed the *Tamaranth*. The next lot could easily be right on top of us.

We dived with scant seconds to spare. Dull flat thuds sounded almost directly above us as a titanic explosion seemed to hammer against our plates like some gigantic fist.

" God ! But that little lot was too close to be healthy,"

I muttered. The others in the control room were grinning feebly as the tension was relieved and we dropped lower into the water. Richards, as usual, said nothing. He seemed to be thinking about something so I left him alone and did not interrupt his thoughts.

To conserve current, all unnecessary lights were extinguished while running submerged. The electric motors had enough work to do driving the submarine through the deeps, without having to supply additional current for indiscriminate lighting.

The sudden change from surface travel to running submerged is one which is difficult to become used to. The steady *thrum* of the diesels merges almost instantly into the quiet purr of the electric motors which are almost impossible to hear unless one concentrates on them. They tend to form a background noise, fading into a dull hum.

But even more difficult to become used to than this change of sound, is the sudden cessation of vibration. The cutting off of the swaying, bouncing motion of a submarine on the surface and the hemmed-in sensation as the water closes about the vessel, dragging it down to the depths.

Movements seem easy and peculiarly effortless. The ponderous shifting of the swell fades to little more than a gentle side to side motion which is strangely soothing.

Richards, with his eyes glued to the eyepiece of the periscope, continued to watch the destroyer now falling rapidly astern. The dull thudding of falling shells and depth charges faded into the distance.

We were both a little surprised and relieved at the fact that we had managed to slip away without any serious damage. It would have been more to our liking if we had been able to remain in the vicinity long enough to witness the demise of both ships, but that was too dangerous. The destroyer, although in a sinking condition, with probably less than an hour to remain afloat, was still a formidable opponent and Richards decided, quite rightly, that discretion was the better part of valour.

Once out of immediate danger, those who were not on duty were ordered below to their bunks to conserve oxygen. In these waters, there was no telling how long we would be forced to run submerged.

Being one of them, I made my way forward to the Messroom. The silence was almost complete. Here and there, above the muted whisper of the electric motors, it was possible to discern the sound of snoring from the seamen's bunks.

It was a tiring existence at sea, more so perhaps than in a surface craft. The dull monotony hung on everybody when there was nothing doing, which occurred most of the time and in addition to this, there was the fact that only when surfaced did we get any fresh air.

Taking off my tunic, I lay down on the bunk and closed my eyes in preparation for sleep. Normally, it did not take me long to fall asleep. The arduous duties were sufficient to tire both brain and body to the point of exhaustion.

This time, however, my mind was so filled with flashing

thoughts that sleep did not come immediately. I lay awake thinking of the struggling figures I had seen momentarily, silhouetted against the crimson glare of burning petroleum as the tanker had exploded in a sheet of flame.

Running figures that were men and young boys like those on board the *Tamaranth*, scurrying like ants, flinging themselves into the flame-shot water in a blind attempt to escape the raging inferno that lay beneath them. A powder-keg on a gigantic scale, ready to blow itself sky-high at a moment's notice.

Hell, they didn't stand much of a chance on board those tankers. It was a fool's job, I reflected idly. One which no sane man would take on. But then, there were those who said the same about our jobs.

There were so many things that could happen on board a submarine, especially when travelling submerged. Depth charges dropped in a diamond pattern around us by a destroyer, following us by hydrophone effect caused by our revolving propellers.

The sudden bursting of steel plates. The crushing pressure of tons of water pouring into the watertight compartments, bubbling, drowning, sweeping everything before it. Sometimes, you were lucky, luckier than you had any right to be. It turned out to be one of the other compartments that received the full force of the sea pouring through a breech in the outer hull.

Sometimes, there was nothing anyone could do as the

submarine, buckled by the titanic force of underwater explosions, took a nose-dive to the ocean bed, where the tremendous water pressure flattened the outer hull like a pancake.

It was with these thoughts running uncomfortably through my brain that I eventually fell into an uneasy, dreamless sleep.

V

Journey Back

THE following morning when I finally woke from a fathomless sleep, we were still running submerged. The electric motors hummed quietly to themselves as I made my way aft to the control room. The Commander was already there. At times, seeing him calmly giving his orders, I wondered when he ever slept himself.

Inwardly, he seemed to be in a bad temper, although this was something he kept from the men. There had been nothing in sight since we had left the tanker and its attendant destroyer. The radio operator had been listening out on any wavelength the enemy might be expected to use, but so far had picked up nothing to indicate whether either of the ships had eventually sunk.

" There should be something coming through any time," he remarked with a forced casualness. " They can't hope to keep a thing like this quiet for long. Not unless they're using some wavelength we know nothing about—and that's highly unlikely."

"Think they could both have gone down so quickly there was no time to send any warning of the attack?"

Richards shook his head after a momentary pause. "I doubt it. Sending a warning would be the first thing they'd do. The radio operator would stand by his post unless the torpedoes struck the radio room."

"That's possible," I agreed.

"If that happened, it must have been a damned lucky fluke on our part." Richards gave a tight grin. The thought seemed to improve his temper slightly.

At nine o'clock, with the horizon still completely clear, we surfaced, the *Tamaranth* planing upwards through the water under perfect control. It appeared that the near misses from the destroyer's fire the previous night had not affected her performance.

"Better recharge the batteries while we have the chance," observed Richards. "We'll post a couple of lookouts too. You never know when we might get a visit from the Luftwaffe in these waters. I did hear early this morning that the *Warspite* and some destroyers had sunk nine German destroyers at Narvik yesterday. If it's true, we can expect some retaliation."

"We're ready for them if they come," I said quietly.

"I wouldn't be too sure of that," he observed grimly. "So far we haven't come under concentrated air attack. It's something I don't relish in the least. We've got a couple of anti-aircraft guns I know, but they still have the advantage over us."

During the early afternoon, smoke was spotted to the north-west, approaching rapidly. We dived and crept towards it, every man at his action stations, every water-tight compartment closed up.

Cautiously, Richards raised the periscope and peered through it.

"Whoever she is, she seems to be steaming a perfectly regular course," he said at length, clamping his lips into a tight line across the middle of his features. "Can't identify her from here. She could be a neutral. In fact, it's more than likely."

"What makes you think so, sir?"

"She must know she's in water likely to be inhabited by submarines. If she had a guilty conscience, she'd be steering the usual zig-zag course. Can't see any signs of guns. Looks just like a cargo ship to me. Nationality unknown. We'll go just a little bit closer. All torpedo tubes stand by."

There was another lengthy period of peering intently through the periscope. Finally, he stood away and motioned me forward.

"Take a look and let me know what you think," he said.

The view seen through the periscope was one of a circular patch of sea and sky, occasionally obliterated by a washing of sea-water over the external lens. The distant ship was almost at the intersection of the cross-wires. She was steaming leisurely across the field of view, belching black smoke from her solitary funnel, trailing it like a beard across the sky.

It was impossible to make out her name. She could have been a German hoping to pass herself off as a neutral in the hope of slipping through our blockade. On the other hand, she could just as easily be a genuine neutral and if that were the case, it would be a stupid move on our part to attack her.

" Well ? "

The Lieutenant-Commander's voice broke in on my thoughts. He came closer and stood beside me, searching my face.

" It's damnably difficult to tell," I muttered, taking my face from the eyepiece. " She could be either. What do you intend to do ? "

" What can we do ? We'll have to let her go. I can't risk taking her any closer just in case it is a German ship, hoping to lure us into a trap. On the other hand, I can't very well put a torpedo into her in case she's a neutral. Then there'd be hell to pay."

We let her go and watched the black cloud of smoke vanish over the lip of the horizon. It had been a difficult decision to make, but under the circumstances, it was the only one.

Another wait. We had almost reached the maximum length of our patrol. Soon it would be time to turn and retrace our steps back to Base. So far, it had been only moderately successful. A troop ship, a tanker and a destroyer. And of the three, the tanker and destroyer were debatable, although it seemed impossible that either could possibly make harbour in their sinking condition.

" Looks as though these waters are deserted," muttered Richards. " If it's true that the Jerries have invaded Norway and Denmark, and there seems no possible doubt about it, we ought to be in the middle of their shipping lanes. Instead, what have we seen lately ? Nothing but a suspected neutral and we couldn't afford to get close enough to it to make out the name. Seems to me we'll go back virtually empty-handed."

" Could be that they're only travelling at night to reduce the risk of being spotted," I suggested.

" If that's the case, we can't afford to wait. We're low on fuel as it is. If we don't spot anything before to-night, we'll have to quit this area and make our way back."

" A pity," I agreed. We had set out with high hopes, but the eternal waiting for something to appear began to get on our nerves. Slowly, we edged our way north-wards, keeping some fifteen miles from the twisting coast-line of Norway. Every position on board was closed up, the torpedo tubes clear and ready.

Shortly before four o'clock, our vigilance was rewarded by the sight of a plume of smoke on the horizon, moving across our path.

" It's beginning to look as though our luck's in again," muttered Richards gleefully. " Perhaps this is where we add a little to our total."

We surged forward, running at periscope depth, the electric motors driving us forward at the maximum nine knots. The sea seemed quite calm now after the previous storms and the sky was perfectly clear with small patches of cloud low down in the east.

" You'd better take over, Lieutenant," he said quietly, turning to me. " We'll take her in as close as possible this time, without being detected. She's moving quite slowly, so we should be able to catch up with her without any trouble. Must be well down in the water, this one."

Gradually, we approached and tried to work ourselves into a suitable attacking position. The light sea, running before a slight south-easterly breeze was just sufficient to cause running white-capped waves to foam around us, thus making it doubly difficult for any enemy to spot the tell-tale track of a periscope.

" What the devil is he playing at ? " I muttered.

" Something wrong, Number One ? " Richards was at my side in an instant.

" Not really, sir. I just can't seem to make him out clearly. Must be spray on the periscope unless— "

Quite suddenly, I saw things clearly, as though a film had dropped from my eyes. There was not one ship in the field of view, but two ! One, a little behind the other, was overlapping sufficiently to make the image seem blurred.

" Two of them ? " muttered Richards when I told him. " Here ! Let me take a look at this."

He glued his eye to the periscope and sucked in his cheeks thoughtfully. There was a strange glint in his eyes as he turned towards me. " Looks as though we arrived here in the nick of time for that poor b——d of a cargo ship," he observed.

" Seems as though she's just foul of a Jerry destroyer. They're too busy engaged in shelling her to take any notice of us. We should be able to get within killing range and put a torpedo into them before they know what's hit them.

" But we'll have to hurry if we're to prevent that other ship from going to the bottom. All forward tubes ready ! "

The acknowledgment was almost immediate. The torpedomen had been waiting for this opportunity for the past couple of hours. Now that it had arrived, they would not be found wanting.

With extreme caution, we approached the scene of conflict. Several shells from the German destroyer had already struck the tanker which was identified as Norwegian although she was not yet in a sinking condition. It was obvious however, that unless we did something, and quickly, she would be sent to the bottom.

Richards wasted no time. Scarcely had we positioned ourselves into a favourable site when he gave the order to fire Numbers One and Four tubes.

His voice sounded more high-pitched than normal as he rapped out the command. It was a sure sign that he was excited. We remained at periscope depth as he watched the track of the torpedo. The enemy destroyer remained on her course, unconscious of the fact that destruction raced towards her on the end of a thin track, scarcely visible.

Tension mounted to fever pitch as the seconds were counted off. Had the torpedoes reached their mark? Would the gremlins which always accompanied them on their voyage prove to be good or bad? If they missed their target, we should have given our position away. It was the simplest thing in the world for a trained lookout to pinpoint the position of a submarine from the torpedo track sufficiently accurately for depth charges to be dropped and do some damage.

The torpedoes seemed to be taking a hell of a time. We had almost given up counting in disgust when the first explosion rocked the ship and sent me staggering against the Commander.

It was followed a split second later by the sound of the second detonation. Richards rubbed his hand together. He was smiling broadly.

"I thought I'd misjudged the speed of that destroyer," he said quickly.

I peered through the periscope. How far off misjudging it was plain to see. The first of the torpedoes had struck the ship cleanly amidships, the other slightly astern. Her guns had ceased firing on the Norwegian, but so far no shells had been thrown in our general direction.

"Probably wondering where the hell those torpedoes came from," grinned Richards. "Can't say I blame them. I'd like to know that if I were in their shoes."

"What do we do now? Give them another torpedo for luck, or chance surfacing and use the gun?"

"There's still a hell of a lot of fight left in her, if you want my opinion," muttered Richards. "It might be better to put another torpedo into her, just to be on the safe side."

Five minutes after the third torpedo had exploded in a crashing of crimson-edged flame, the enemy destroyer was listing badly to starboard. She was going down by the stern and already waves were washing over her.

"Any signals going out from her?" yelled Richards.

After a brief pause, the reply came back. The destroyer had begun signalling the instant after the first two torpedoes had struck, but had ceased transmitting almost immediately after the third had exploded. The reason seemed fairly obvious. The third detonation had either destroyed her radio room, or shattered the aerial completely.

It was hopeless to think of coming to the surface and engaging the enemy in a gun duel. Sinking as she was, she could still deliver a knock-out punch from that distance and there was no sense in taking foolish chances.

The destroyer was now blazing furiously, sending up clouds of red-tinted smoke. Several of the boats were being lowered and we could see them being rowed quickly from the sinking ship.

The profile of the ship stood out against the skyline as she began to settle by the stern. She sank quickly. All three torpedoes appeared to have exploded just below the water line. Half an hour later, there was little of her remaining above the surface.

Nothing to fear from her guns now, the Commander decided to surface and investigate the position of the Norwegian ship now making her way under her own steam. Slowly, the *Tamaranth* planed through the water to the surface.

Richards clambered up the swaying ladder, motioning me to follow him. An icy wave slapped over the wind-break of the bridge. Seeing it coming, I ducked and felt it splash over me. Richards caught it full in the face. He glanced up, spluttering and cursing loudly.

We passed astern of the sinking destroyer, watching her slide beneath the encroaching waves. The survivors were heading towards the distant Norwegian shore. Most of them appeared to have got into the boats.

Several seamen crowded the rails of the Norwegian cargo steamer as we slid alongside some fifty yards away. Some were waving their caps excitedly. All looked pleased to see us.

" Wonder if anyone there speaks English," muttered Richards taking the megaphone into his hand. " We'll just have to trust to luck otherwise."

He shouted across to the ship. " Anybody there speak English ? "

We waited, bracing ourselves as the submarine began to roll slightly. There was a spreading wash reaching outward from the German destroyer as she went under for the last time. A lather of foam smacked against the bridge and washed over us.

"Somebody coming forward now, sir," I said, pointing.

Apparently, it was the Skipper of the ship. He pushed his way towards the damaged bridge, megaphone in his hand. A once-white bandage had been wrapped around his forehead, standing out in startling contrast to his uniform. He raised the megaphone to his lips and shouted back.

"I understand English, Commander. Pleased to see you here. We thought we were finished until you showed up. Good show!"

"Thanks." Richards yelled the word back through the amplifying throat of the megaphone. "Glad to have been of help. Can you manage to get to port in your condition? If not, we can take some of your men on board."

"We can manage under our own steam, thanks. The engine room is undamaged. Most of it seems to have been confined to the superstructure. We have the fires under control."

"Where are you bound for?"

"Any of the British ports, Commander. We slipped out of Stavanger last night before the Germans could stop us. We were lucky. Several of the other ships have been taken over."

"Good luck then. I hope you make it."

"Thank you, Commander."

The sea washed and sparkled over our bows as we turned away. There was no sign of the enemy destroyer apart from scattered wreckage on the heavy swell and a patch of oil drifting on top of the water. We saw no survivors in the water, although they could not all have got away in the boats.

VI

Base

FOR three days after our dramatic and timely meeting with the Norwegian cargo steamer, we saw nothing. Gradually, we worked our way westwards, away from the German shipping lanes around the Norwegian and Danish coasts. We were entering relatively unfrequented waters.

But if there were no surface craft, there still remained the constant menace of the Luftwaffe, patroling the sea. Twice on the third day, we were forced to crash-dive to escape the ttentions of a low-flying bomber. The last time, it seen d impossible that we had not been spotted, but oddly enc gh, no bombs began to fall and we breathed freely again.

During the rly morning of the fourth day, however, while we were l some hundred miles from the coast of Britain, our goc luck deserted us. We had dived to reload the empty ubes in the hope that something was bound to appear after so long a wait.

At 04.00 hours, the peaceful tranquillity of travelling

submerged was shattered by the sound of several explosions almost directly above us, slightly astern. Those
of the crew resting in their bunks, scrambled to action
stations, still blinking their eyes, half-asleep, cursing bitterly
at the sudden change of events.

"What is it, sir?" I asked.

Richards shook his head dubiously. "Too early to tell
at the moment. Seems to be nothing coming in from the
hydrophone operator. Can't see very well how it can
possibly be a German destroyer. We'd have picked him
up before this."

He turned away and began to issue his orders in an
undertone, his voice subdued. There was no point in
taking chances. If there was a destroyer or some other
such craft on top of us, they would be straining every nerve
and instrument in trying to detect us.

A pause, followed by a further salvo of explosions.
Nearer this time. Something was definitely on our tail
and refused to be shaken off.

Finally, Richards gave the order: "Climb to periscope
depth."

We planed upwards slowly, cautiously. It could be
anything. There was not a sound in the boat. Men
worked mechanically, sweating a little from the heat and
the tension. The helpless sensation of claustrophobia
which affects submarine men at times such as that, made it
difficult to think properly.

Strange that we had heard nothing from the hydrophone
operator, I thought; he was normally the first person to
pick up the proximity of a surface craft.

We levelled off at periscope depth and Richards peered

through the eyepiece, turning the periscope gently in its well.

" Can't see a bloody thing," he said finally, biting his lower lip.

" There has to be something," I muttered uneasily. It was uncanny, knowing that something had fallen and exploded within yards of us and yet there was nothing which could have originated the mischief.

" Still can't see a— " He broke off with a muttered oath. There was something of a powerful dynamo about him as he snapped: " Down periscope ! Flood ! "

There were little beads of perspiration standing out on his furrowed brow as the periscope slid its shining length out of sight into the well.

The alarm signal was still ringing through the boat as he turned to me and said: " No wonder we couldn't pick him up. He's up there, circling this spot, waiting for another chance to drop his load of bombs."

" An aircraft." Realisation dawned on me in a moment of blinding clarity.

" Exactly. And unless I miss my guess, there may be two of them, taking it in turns to hunt us down. There's still plenty of moonlight to help them pick us out. The water's just about as flat as a mirror."

" Hellfire."

In the minutes that followed, nerves were stretched to breaking point. Men hurried about their tasks in a kind of noiseless haste, anticipating each other's movements and requirements. Fear showed at times in their faces. Not the fear of being bombed, that was something they could expect and face; but the ever-present fear of going down to the bottom in the steel coffin which was the *Tamaranth*.

That thought must have been at the back of everyone's mind during the entire patrol, but nobody had wanted to be the first to mention it, to bring it out into the open.

The long seconds passed as though drawn out into immense proportions and became minutes. No more bombs seemed to be heading in our direction and we began to breathe more freely. For the moment, it seemed, we were safe.

" We'll stay down here for another half hour and give them a chance to go away," said Richards quietly. He wiped his forehead with the sleeve of his tunic. Half an hour later, we planed slowly to periscope depth for another quick look around. Richards, peering through the eye-piece, withdrew his head sharply with a sudden shout.

The aircraft had been wise to our little manoeuvre. They were still there and Richards, looking out had seen one of them in the action of coming in for a bombing run. The *Tamaranth* went into a steep crash-dive. Men staggered against bulkheads and from the galley came the crash of falling dishes and the sound of something heavy falling against one of the walls.

" Better go and see what that was," suggested Richards, turning to one of the men.

A few moments later, the man was back with the news that another of the men had been thrown violently against the wall by the angle of dive and was unconscious.

While he was removed for his injuries to be attended to, the remainder of us waited with bated breath, listening in the intense silence. One minute went by then another. Then came the sudden *crumping* of explosions near at hand.

The *Tamaranth* seemed to career madly as though struck by some giant underwater fist. Richards staggered and

half fell as she threatened to keel over. Behind me, someone out of sight, slithered on the metal floor and crashed
against the wall, bringing down a shower of small instru-
ments with him.

A split second later, the lights went out. There came
another explosion, louder than all of the others put together. Glass was being shattered somewhere nearby.
One of the men was cursing steadily and fluently in the
darkness and a pocket torch flashed on, probing the
blackness in my direction. I realised it was Richards.

There was a streak of blood on his temple just above
the left eye and he was breathing heavily. Someone else
was moaning with a terrible softness a couple of feet
away.

" God, how much longer do we have to wait for the
emergency lighting ? " Richards swore quickly between his
teeth.

A long moment fled before the emergency lighting came
on and we were able to see clearly again. The man who
had fallen against the wall, still lay in a huddled heap.
There was blood on the side of his face where he had
fallen against an outjutting metal section.   He was
unconscious.

Someone made a move towards him, then stopped as
another detonation slammed against us from above.   The
submarine seemed to drop several feet before steadying,
but perhaps that was more my imagination than anything
else.

Richards was the first to pull himself together.   He
stepped to the intercom. "I want a report from every
compartment, of the ship," he snapped. " Any damage
done and how badly we've been hit.   That's all."

" We may as well know the worst from the very beginning," he added grimly, turning to the rest of us.

" We can't expect to get away with it every time, sir," muttered someone reflectively.

" No. But that was closer than I like it. Too close to be really healthy."

There were no more explosions and as the minutes ticked by, information began to filter in. Reports came from all stations. Everything was still tight and no water was coming in, although some superficial damage had been done. Several men had been injured slightly by the force of the explosions, but that was all.

For the best part of an hour, we cruised slowly away from the scene, remaining at maximum depth. There came another flurry of bombs, but they were quite distant and it was comforting to know that we had put a goodly slice of distance between ourselves and the watchful aircraft.

At the end of the hour, we surfaced. It was almost dawn. A faint rim of grey light had appeared on the edge of the sea, low down in the east. Even as we watched, it appeared to brighten perceptibly.

Richards clambered stiffly onto the bridge and stood with his hands resting on the windbreak. As he had said earlier, the sea was at its calmest. Scarcely a ripple distorted the surface of the water, save where the bow of the *Tamaranth* clove it into a splashing of white that swirled and bubbled around her smooth length.

" Nothing in sight," said the Commander at last. He rubbed his cheek reflectively with one finger. " Just as well perhaps. " We've all had enough excitement for one day at least."

I nodded. In the west, the moon was already sinking, throwing a last, departing glow across the water. The stars were already fading, slipping out of sight one by one. Forward of us, the lookouts were dark ghostly figures silhouetted against the grey brilliance of the oncoming dawn.

Soon it was bright enough to make out their features. It would be daylight soon. To the man of a submarine, this magic hour between night and day is something peculiarly sacred. It is more than the beginning of a new day, more even than the fact that we had survived to see it break.

It meant that there was an end to peering with sleep-dimmed eyes through a periscope that picked out nothing but darkness and an occasional flash of white foam as a wave washed itself against the periscope glass. It meant that from now on, we would be able to spot our quarry at a sufficient distance to manoeuvre ourselves into a favourable attacking position and still retain the important element of surprise.

Richards seemed to feel some of this too, for he drew in a deep breath and leaned his weight forward onto his elbows, staring at the sea. His face was serious and I had a vague idea what he was thinking about. Perhaps he was remembering the ear-splitting explosion which had rocked the tanker a few days earlier before sending it to the bottom. The sight of boats pulling away from it in a desperate, urgent hurry, striving to get out of the immediate area before a second explosion killed them where they were.

Maybe he was wondering, as no doubt the rest of us were wondering, just what was got out of all this slaughtering of men and wrecking of ships. Why we were at war in the first place and how long it would be before sanity returned to a world torn by strife and bitter hatred.

Everyone seemed to have gone insane now that this man, Hitler, had embarked on his reign of terror and bloodshed. From what we had been able to learn from the wireless messages we picked up occasionally, the enemy were making rapid strides in Norway and Denmark although Allied landings had been made on the coast.

Whether these would fare well, still remained a matter of conjecture. It seemed doubtful. The enemy had too strong a grip on Europe to be shaken that easily.

For the remainder of that morning, we remained on the surface. The diesels continued to drive us forward at close on fifteen knots but by midday, a breeze sprang up and rollers came slapping against the bow of the ship. Soon, it was quite heavy going. Still not a ship in sight.

Far to the south-west, there were the heavy black curtains of a rain-squall hanging low on the horizon, but luckily, it was moving away and Richards decided not to submerge. The first gulls made their appearance. We were not far from land now, if the signs were anything to go by.

Time and again, the lookouts reported something on the horizon, but just as often it turned out to be something else and not smoke. Spirits began to sink a little.

Then, without warning, a dark shape appeared out of the lowering clouds, heading straight towards us. The starboard lookout spotted it first and pointed, with a shout of warning.

Richards turned his head quickly and peered at it through the binoculars. At first, I thought it was a Beaufighter, then quickly changed my mind as Richards yelled :

" Anti-aircraft guncrews on deck. Hurry ! "

Matthews and Parsons, the gunners, still in their teens came clambering up the narrow ladder, pulled themselves out of the conning-tower and raced towards the small anti-aircraft guns aft of the bridge. Others followed.

" There's no time to dive." shouted Richards hoarsely. " He'd sink us before we had a chance. We'll have to have it out with him whether we like it or not. Everything ready ? "

" All ready, sir." Parsons nodded. The gun was already pointed at the diving aircraft. He came low out of the sun which explained why he had not been sighted earlier.

" Open fire as soon as he's in range." Ordered the Commander.

The port gun opened up almost immediately although the shells went wide of their mark. It was impossible to bring the four-incher to bear.

" Here she comes." I found myself yelling the warning instinctively. It was totally unnecessary.

The starboard gun joined in too a moment later. It was unfortunate that the aircraft had not been spotted sooner. We would have stood a little more chance of survival under the surface. But that could not be helped now. We had to make the best of an unfortunate job.

A few seconds elapsed. The guns were still spitting their fire at the incoming bomber, but with little visible effect. He did not seem to swerve by so much as one degree from his course.

" Bombs dropping." Yelled one of the lookouts. Glancing up, I caught a fragmentary glimpse of the black blob that dropped from the belly of the plane and seemed to hang suspended almost indefinitely in mid-air before suddenly hurtling towards us at an incredible speed.

It was the first time I had actually seen a bomb coming towards me like that. All other times we had been running submerged. The effect was stunning. One minute, the bomb seemed to be hanging several hundred feet in the air, a scant couple of yards from the plane.

The next, it had hurtled towards the submarine, splashing into the water less than twenty yards away on the port bow. Instinctively, I ducked and Richards followed suit an instant later. The guns were still hammering away madly as the plane rocketed over and began to climb steeply to our rear.

The next instant, the water on the port bow seemed to glow with a sudden flash of underwater brilliance, then gather itself into a snowy mountain of foam-edged spray and hurl itself at the heavens. A tumult of water poured against the bridge, rushing over us, drenching us to the skin.

"He'll be coming round again in a few moments." yelled the Commander in my ear. "The next time we may not be so lucky. Hell! What do those gunners think they're doing back there?"

I glanced round trying to pick out the circling aircraft against the cloud-flecked sky. It was not easy. Finally, I managed to locate it and saw with a thrill of surprise that it was trailing a long plume of black smoke from one engine.

Richards saw it a moment later. "He's been hit!" he muttered. "I don't think he'll be bothering us again. Damned good shooting."

We watched through the binoculars as the plane limped

away to the east. Barely ten seconds later, however, she seemed to pause in flight, then tilt forward towards the sea going down in a rising column of red-shot smoke. A sparkle of petrol-driven flame spread rapidly over the surface of the sea where she struck and a pall of smoke hung over the scene like a funeral pyre.

The trip back was uneventful after that. We spotted several ships as we approached the Shetlands, but they all turned out to be friendly or neutral. Three days later, we arrived back in Rothesay, fourteen days after we had set out on patrol.

VII

Second Operation

THE *Tamaranth* was in dock longer than had at first been thought necessary. Damage from the bombing raid had caused buckling of the outer plates and in places, it was found imperative to carry out major repairs.

Because of this, the submarine was laid up almost a month longer than had been intended and it was early July before she was ready again.

When we finally boarded her, it was to find that several of the old members of the crew were no longer with us and there were new faces to remember and names to attach to them. But the Lieutenant-Commander was still there, as rugged as ever, determined that nothing was going to keep him in dock a moment longer than was necessary.

Simpson, the new Engineer Officer was an old hand on submarines having been on them as long as Richards,

Then there was Masson, the Chief Telegraphist and
Templeton the hydrophone operator. All new and there
were others, but their names would have to be memorised
in due course when there was time for such things.

Since we had last gone out on patrol, much had happened
in Europe. Events had taken a decided turn for the worse.
The enemy seemed to be making rapid strides on all fronts.
Nowhere was any stand being made against him.

Norway lay in the iron grip of the German High Command. Denmark had been overthrown with only a token
show of resistance. Early in May, Holland and Belgium
had been invaded, there being no warning given. In the
usual Hilterite method of waging war, German armoured
Divisions had poured across the frontiers, swarming into
the Low Countries.

A month later, almost to the day, Italy had declared war
on the Allies and we were forced to extend our area of
operations. Six days later, the French had collapsed
before the German onslaught.

We were now fighting alone.

*   *   *

Something was undoubtedly in the wind. On shore it
had been glaringly obvious. The last few weeks had seen
repairs to the *Tamaranth* carried through at an incredible
speed.

Our destination this time was not the mine-strewn waters of the Norwegian fiords, but the smoother coast of France. A France largely occupied by enemy forces. The strictest secrecy was maintained throughout the whole of the pre-parations. There were several other submarines of the "T" class moored at Rothesay, two of which put to sea before we left. We heard nothing concerning their desti-nation.

After the long-endured quiet of shore leave, it was good to stand on the bridge and feel the wind blowing clean and fresh into our faces. We slipped our moorings quietly during the early morning shortly after dawn, and headed southwards down the coast.

We passed shipping in plenty, but it was all friendly and we ignored it completely. Occasionally, we saw the coast, but for the most part, we kept well out to sea. Once we were spotted by a low-flying Sunderland which buzzed down on us to identify a submarine moving in British waters, but we were obviously considered friendly for it zoomed off a few minutes later.

" They're pretty hot in these parts," observed Richards cynically. " Good job we weren't a U-Boat, otherwise he'd have been on to us like a flash."

" It's comforting to know they're there, anyway," I said.

Richards nodded and turned back to his contemplation of the surrounding area. There were certain mine-fields strewn about the coast and it was vitally important to know of them in advance. Most of our time was taken up with watching for them, checking our position every thirty minutes.

The weather which had been blustery for July, improved considerably during the afternoon as we worked our way southwards. The wind dropped until it was barely perceptible.

By nightfall, the weather was as perfect as could be wished. The coastline which had hovered on the horizon during the day, faded into a deep purple haze as the sun disappeared and Edwards, the navigator, was able to get his first star sights.

It promised to be a fine night, one of many which were to follow during our trip. The sunset was one of unimaginable colours; reds and greens and yellows, all blending together in the west where long banks of cloud spread lines of flame across the darkening sky.

Two days later we were off the coast of France and in enemy held waters. From now on, we could expect attacks from both sea and air. Through the binoculars, it was just possible to make out the town of Coutainville. We were within three sea miles of it and it seemed strange to think that already the heel of the conqueror lay across it.

We had, at the time, no way of telling the routes the enemy shipping was using. Edwards was of the opinion that it moved along the French coast to Cherbourg.

Richards, on the other hand, insisted that it travelled direct for Cherbourg passing near the Channel Islands.

Just what was the situation? At the time, it was any-body's guess. One opinion was just as feasible as the other. By noon, we were moving slowly northwards, hugging the French coast but keeping well out of sight and range of the coastal batteries.

For three days we remained in the same area, running submerged most of the time, but spotting nothing. Per-haps the navigator had been right, after all; and the enemy shipping was moving across to the north of us. Two or three times, it seemed we might possibly be in luck, but each time it turned out to be a false alarm.

Once a speedboat heading towards the coast, coming from some direction we were unable to fathom; and the other instance, a small group of fishing boats, apparently going about their lawful duties. We decided to leave them alone. Attacking them would give our position away immediately and so far, we had remained undiscovered. Also, these men on board the fishing vessels were un-doubtedly Frenchmen, our Allies, and we would gain nothing by sinking them. We might even gain some unwanted publicity, because the enemy would not hesitate to use it as propaganda against us.

The weather remained fine, the sea calm; but it also brought out the enemy air patrols. We were constantly on the dive to avoid the unwelcome attention of low-flying planes carrying out reconnaissance sweeps over the French coastal waters.

The Commander's temper grew steadily worse as time went on and we cruised impotently in an area which was supposed to be a rich ground for submarines. Had the enemy shipping lanes been altered for some reason unknown to us ? It was possible. These things happened at times for no reason at all.

Towards evening on the eighth day, smoke was sighted to the north, heading in our general direction. The Officer of the Watch called down the conning tower, his voice sharp with excitement. Only twenty-three years old, it was his first trip on submarines.

" Commander on the bridge ! "

By the time Richards and I had reached the bridge, hurrying up the swaying metal-runged ladder, the ship had already approached to within ten thousand yards. Still outside the range of our torpedoes, but the distance was diminishing gradually.

" Think she's spotted ue yet, sir ? " asked the Officer of the Watch, trying to make his voice sound casual and not succeeding too well.

" Too soon to tell. She certainly isn't acting that way. Seems to be keeping to her original course. Prepare to dive ! "

The lookouts skipped down the conning tower and vanished into the control room. Lieutenant-Commander Richards was the last to come below. There was a hollow clang as the hatch was closed and secured. Meanwhile, everything in the *Tamaranth* was going according to plan.

At periscope depth, the submarine straightened out and came onto a level keel. Seconds seemed to stretch themselves out into individual eternities as the periscope moved up slowly from its well.

"Everybody quiet," ordered Richards tautly. This was our first possible victim; our first chance of a kill.

In the control room, there was no sound whatever. It was as though every man was holding his breath as Richards took his first look at the approaching vessel. A few moments later, it was possible to hear the sound of his propellers.

"All tubes ready."

The acknowledgment came back almost instantly.

"Tubes ready, sir."

The *Tamaranth* possessed ten twenty-one inch torpedo tubes, six in the bows and four aft which made her a formidable foe.

Richards, his face furrowed with concentration, lined up on the unsuspecting victim. There was nothing hurried in his movements. His hands were steady and sure as he watched the ship through the enhanced vision of the periscope.

Almost casually, it seemed, he gave the awaited order to fire two of the tubes. We all felt the imperceptible shudder as the torpedoes started on their way towards the target.

"She's a cargo vessel of about five thousand tons, I'd guess," muttered the Commander finally, taking his eye from the periscope. He seemed quite unconcerned.

We waited, listening for the muffled explosions which

would tell us that the torpedoes had reached their mark. The seconds ticked by. Then, when we had almost given up hope, they came. A dull, distant booming roar followed closely by a second, louder this time.

Immediately, Richards was at the periscope. He passed on the information in a hurried whisper, hoarse-voiced.

" The first got her aft of the funnel. The second must have lopped off her stern. She's settling quickly. God knows what she must have been carrying. Oil, probably. It's a bloody inferno. There can't have been many survivors."

A few moments later, he stood back and motioned me towards the periscope. Through the eyepiece, slipping gently off the crosswires, I could make out the glaring fury of the sinking ship. I heard the radio operator telling the Commander that no signals had been broadcast from the stricken ship.

Apparently, there had been no warning before the radio room had been destroyed by the first explosion. Once again, we were in luck. Had any message got through, we would have had destroyers on our necks within minutes

The vessel settled quickly into the water, her bows lifted clear into the air as she slid under. Fires were still raging in the holds and even as I watched, there came a sudden, thunderous explosion, greater than the rest. Glowing splinters of metal ploughed upwards into the air, hanging motionless for a breathless instant, before showering down into the sea. The *Tamaranth* trembled in every plate as the underwater detonation wave reached her.

"What the devil happened there?" asked Richards anxiously.

"The cargo must have exploded," I said, without taking my eyes off the scene. "She's blown up completely. Nothing left of her now except some wreckage."

Coming forward, Richards peered for a long moment through the eyepiece, then nodded his head slowly. I could understand how he was feeling. There had been men on board that vessel. Men such as ourselves, with their own individual lives, their loves and hates.

Perhaps many of them had been married with families, like the Commander himself. And now, where were they? Floating lifeless on the sea, blown into mutilated obscurity by the titanic force of the explosion.

Such were the fortunes of war. If that vital cargo had managed to get through to the enemy, it would have been used against us, our own families. Daily, the Luftwaffe was bombing London and Coventry and the other towns and cities of the British Isles. Men and women and children were dying in hundreds as bombs crashed down from the heavens, burying them beneath piles of rubble and falling masonry.

No, the sensation of pity which I had felt at first, seeing the ship go down, did not last long. The men on board her had known the risks they were taking in these waters. They were professional fighting men like ourselves. Not like the innocent women and children in the cities and towns.

"We'll surface and see if we can pick up any survivors," said Richards suddenly, his voice sharp. "There may be some and it's possible that we can gain some information from them."

" Think that's wise, sir ? " I asked. " Someone may have spotted that ship. She'd have been visible for miles. Maybe even on the coast— "

Richards rubbed his cheek characteristically. " It's hardly likely," he muttered finally. " She went down within minutes and I think we can discard the possibility of her having sent out any warning signals."

Stealthily, we climbed to the surface. It was almost dark. The sky was quite clear; there was no sign of the cargo ship. Tirelessly, the lookouts, standing braced against the swaying up-and-down motion of the boat, searched the growing darkness through their night glasses.

At first, there was nothing. Standing on the bridge, it was difficult to make out objects in the water. Dark things would sweep by, carried along by the rush of water past the bows, but inevitably, they turned out to be drifting bits of wreckage, twisted into shapeless masses by the explosion.

" Something up ahead, sir." The starboard lookout shouted excitedly, pointing.

" Keep it in sight," ordered Richards harshly.

Suddenly, drifting towards us, carried first on top of a wave, then plunged down into the hollow trough, we spotted a length of driftwood. Clinging to it, we could just make out the shape of a man.

" Careful how you get him on board," yelled Richards. There was no need for him to use a megaphone. The night was quite calm and his voice carried to the two men who had tumbled out of the conning tower and were making their way quickly, but cautiously, towards the starboard bow of the *Tamaranth*.

Gingerly, Richards brought the boat alongside as the men leaned over and caught hold of the semi-conscious man in the water. Struggling a little, they managed to haul him on board, dragging him clear of the encroaching waves. The length of driftwood which had saved his life, sped on its way without him, twisting and turning until it was lost to view in the bubbling waters of the wake.

" Take him down below," ordered Richards quietly. He turned to me.

" You'd better take a look at him, Number One." he added. " See how badly hurt he is. If possible, I'd like to question him. He may talk, he may not. But there's always a chance and in a dangerous game such as this, we can't afford to pass anything up. Meanwhile, we'll keep on the lookout for any others there might be."

" I doubt whether there'll be many still alive, sir. " I muttered. That final explosion must have killed any who remained in the vicinity almost outright."

" True enough, I suppose. But we'll give it another twenty minutes or so, unless anyone else puts in an appearance."

I made my way down the steel runged ladder and stood waiting at the bottom while the two rescuers lowered the injured man gently down into the control room.

" Where shall we put him, sir ? "

" Better take him into the wardroom. There'll be more room there. And if we have to dive quickly, we don't want him in the control room."

Carefully, the man was carried forward into the ward-room and laid on one of the bunks. He was moaning softly and sea water, dripping from his soaked clothing ran in tiny puddles on the floor.

" He looks pretty bad, sir," muttered Burton, one of the rescuers. " Think he'll live ? "

" That's difficult to tell at the moment," I said. " Let's take a look at him."

There was a thin streak of blood on the back of his head where it seemed he had either fallen against some object or been hit when the explosion had occurred. How he had managed to hang onto the drifting length of wood, was a mystery. He could not have been more than semi-conscious all of the time, but some instinct had forced him to hold on, not knowing whether rescue would come or not.

Carefully, I removed his shirt. There were several long bruises down the length of his back, running between the shoulder blades. He screamed out loud as I touched them, feeling for any broken bones.

" Any idea what's wrong, sir ? " asked Burton.

" It's worse than I thought." I forced the words out. No longer did I think of the man on the bunk as a German, an enemy. He was just another human being with a shattered spine.

Richards came down a few moments later. He shook his head at my inquiring glance. " Nothing there," he said. " It's getting too dark to pick out anything now. Even if there were any more around to be picked up."

He paused and glanced down at the inert figure on the bunk. " How about him ? Think he'll be able to talk at all ? "

" He may," I began quietly. " But you'll have to ask him all the questions you want very soon, immediately he regains consciousness."

" Why ? What's the matter with him ? Is it as serious as all that ? "

I found myself nodding absently. " I think his spine has been shattered during that explosion." I said tensely. " It's a miracle he's survived this length of time. And how he managed to cling onto that lump of wood is completely beyond me."

" I see," Richard's voice was grim. It sounded oddly loud in the confined space of the wardroom. " Do what you can for him. Let me know if it will be possible to talk with him. We might be able to learn quite a lot."

VIII

SECRET ASSIGNMENT

ONE glance was sufficient to tell that although the man was slowly regaining consciousness, it was impossible for him to live until morning. He was breathing heavily and as I touched his forehead to wipe away some of the blood, he twisted back his lips in a grimace of pain and put up his hands to try to pull mine away.

I turned to Burton. "See if you can get hold of any morphia," I said. "It may help to relieve the pain. Otherwise, he won't be able to stand it when he becomes fully conscious."

The other began to mumble something in German under his breath as Burton went off. After a few moments, his eyes opened and he looked directly at me. For a moment, there was a blank stare in them as he tried to turn his head to look about him.

"You're all right," I said reassuringly. "Just a back wound, that's all."

"Looks as though he can understand you, sir," said the other man, standing by, watching.

As though in answer, the German nodded. " I speak your language," he said through clenched teeth. " What happened on the ship ? " He tried to lift himself up, then stifled on a scream.

"Better lie back and take it easy," I said, holding him down. " You were wounded during the explosion. Must have knocked you about a bit. You were also in the water for the best part of half an hour. Just lie still and we'll have you fixed in no time."

" My back. There is something wrong with my back."

For the first time, there was a look of fear on his face. Not the fear of dying, but of something he didn't quite understand.

He twisted his face awkwardly and looked up at me with an expression of pleading in his eyes. " What is it ? My back—is it broken ? "

"We don't know yet. I don't think so," I lied instinctively, without betraying it on my face.

He sank back at that and appeared to relax somewhat. An instant later, Burton came back with the morphia and a hypodermic. He handed them to me without a word.

" This will make you feel better," I said, rolling back the other's sleeve.

He winced slightly as the needle entered the flesh of his upper arm, but gave no other sign. At first, it began to look as though it would not have the desired effect. Then, gradually, his breathing began to quieten and the taut muscles of his face relaxed.

" That's better," I said under my breath. " He'll probably sleep a little now. I'll stay with him until he wakes. Be ready to warn the Commander as soon as I give the word."

Five minutes later, the sound of the diesels changed to the quiet humming of the electric motors and I knew that we had submerged again. After the sinking of the cargo ship, the Commander would want to get well away from the area before retribution in the shape of enemy destroyers made itself felt.

The hours passed slowly. Several times it seemed that the injured German would wake from the drug-induced sleep, but each time he closed his eyes and relaxed again.

While he was asleep, I examined the remainder of his body for any other injuries but apart from superficial bruising he seemed all right. It was his back that had caught the full shock of the explosion. He had not got long to live; that much was painfully obvious. And it was going to be a hell of a way in which to die.

Twice during the early part of the night we picked up the threshing of propellers, but each time they gradually faded and it was clear that they were not looking for us particularly, although once, shortly before midnight, there came the sound of depth charges exploding a short distance away.

Silence reigned on board the *Tamaranth* until the danger had passed. All men not on duty, went to their bunks and slept.

At 0100 hours, the German stirred, twisted his head convulsively and opened his eyes. Recognition came after a few moments. His lips parted and moved several times before any words came out and I was forced to bend my head to catch what he was saying.

' Where am I ? "

Automatically, he had spoken in his native tongue, but the meaning behind the phrase was obvious.

" You're on board a British submarine," I said quietly.

" Don't you remember ? Your ship was torpedoed last night. We managed to pick you up out of the water; you were hanging on to a piece of wreckage."

He nodded his head slowly and with effort. " I remember," he whispered, licking his lips. " Were there any other survivors ? "

" We searched the area for half an hour," I replied. " But you were the only one we spotted. There may have been others in the boats. They would have made for the mainland. We didn't follow them for obvious reasons."

" No, of course not. I understand." He turned his head away wearily and closed his eyes again. His back did not seem to be troubling him quite so much and for a wild moment, I had the idea that perhaps I had been wrong in the preliminary diagnosis. Then he looked back at me and I saw the beads of sweat standing out on his forehead although the air was quite cold and the greyness of his face.

No. I had not been wrong.

He twisted his mouth in an attempt at a smile. " Funny, I don't seem to be able to feel a thing now," he said, speaking English. He shook his head feebly. There was a far-away look in his eyes.

I turned to Burton. " Better get hold of the Commander if you can."

" Yes, sir."

The other's footsteps sounded loudly on the metal floor as he made his way aft to the control room. During the interval before Richards made his appearance, the injured German tossed and turned on the bunk, mumbling quietly in some form of delirium.

" He seems to be sinking slowly, sir," said Carson, the leading torpedo-man.

" Yes, I'm afraid you're right. Perhaps it's better that way. He must have suffered tremendously since it happened."

I opened my mouth to say something else, but at that moment, the wardroom door opened and the Commander came in. His face was tight and emotionless.

" What is it, Number One ?   Has he come round ? "

I stood up and nodded towards the man on the bunk.

" You'll have to ask your questions quickly, sir. He won't last much longer."

" You're sure ? "

" I'm afraid so, sir. His spine has been damaged very severely."

" You can do nothing for him ? "   It was more of a statement than a question, but I nodded and said:

" There's nothing anybody can do for him now, sir."

" I see.   Very well.   Does he speak English ? "

I nodded in the affirmative and Richards bent over the bunk, speaking softly but urgently to the dying man. For a moment, I thought the other was not going to answer, but finally, his lips moved and he whispered something so quietly, that only the Commander was able to make it out.

A few moments later, the other fell back into a fit of coughing. Slowly, his hand, fumbling for the side of the bunk, as though he were trying to pull himself upright in one last, despairing gasp, relaxed and fell away onto his chest.

Richards straightened. He felt for the other's pulse, then allowed the limp hand to fall back.

He turned slowly. " No use getting any more morphia, Number One," he said tightly. " He's dead. Just too late. I couldn't get anything worthwhile out of him. A pity. We might have been able to find out about their shipping routes, if only he'd talked."

" What do we do with him now, sir ? "

" There's only one thing we can do. He'll be buried at sea with full military honours. It makes no difference because he's one of the enemy."

An hour later, shortly before dawn broke, we surfaced cautiously and took a quick look around. There was nothing in sight and the sky was clear of aircraft. Richards stood stiffly on the bridge as the body of the German seaman, wrapped in a sheet, weighted to carry it below, was brought up into the conning tower.

The dawn was brightening in the east over France as the final words were said over the body before it slipped over the side of the *Tamaranth* and vanished below the waves.

After the brief ceremony, we remained on the surface for a couple of hours, recharging the batteries and allowing fresh, salt air to blow through the submarine. The crew were in a subdued mood after the death of the German seaman. Almost as though it had been an omen. The men who sail in the submarines are, after all, the most superstitious of all sea-going folk.

For two more days, we prowled along the rocky coast-line of enemy-occupied France, keeping a strict lookout, but the sealanes were empty of traffic. Once, cruising on the surface during the early hours of the morning, we came across a wide patch of oil staining the flat surface of the sea, glinting with a million rainbow colours in the brilliant moonlight.

" Looks as though there's been some action here," said Kenniston, the Sub-Lieutenant also on watch. He swept the area with his binoculars, but there was no sign of floating wreckage. Occasionally, bubbles would burst on the surface, so it was evident that something big had gone down and settled almost intact on the bottom.

" Must have been one of the enemy," I said, " so near to the French coast as this."

We passed slowly through the oil, watching it drift past us like an artificial skin on the rippling surface of the sea.

" Unless it was one of our submarines hit by enemy air patrols," muttered Kenniston sombrely.

It was a sobering thought and one which had not entered my mind. There was a tightening of the muscles in the pit of my stomach. We were alone here, miles from any help.

The boat was rolling a bit and there was a heavy swell running. We could not be more than two or three sea miles off shore. It had been the Commander's intention to reconnoitre the area and if the opportunity arose, to attack any enemy shipping which showed itself.

Shortly before dawn, Richards came onto the bridge. There was a slip of paper in his right hand which he held out to me.

" We received this by radio ten minutes ago," he said in reply to my expression of inquiry. " It was in code, so you can guess at its importance."

I glanced down at the directive, whistling through my teeth. If the message was anything to go by, we were assigned an extremely delicate mission. It was straightforward and to the point.

Briefly, we were to proceed to a secret rendezvous, given as a set of figures, to arrive off the French coast at precisely 23.45 hours the next night and pick up a couple of British agents who were being shipped out of occupied France to be taken back to London.

Then followed the signals which were to be given and received from the shore once we reached our rendezvous.

" Do the rest of the crew know about this yet, sir ? " I asked.

Richards shook his head. " No. My orders are to tell nobody apart from yourself until we actually reach our destination."

IX

Rendezvous

DURING the intervening hours, the crew of the *Tamaranth* were kept in a state of growing tension and bewilderment. Twice during the next morning, smoke was spotted on the horizon and Richards made no move to attack, or even to investigate.

It was soon obvious to the men that something important was in the air, although at the time they knew none of the details. Perhaps they suspected something, but nothing was said, and it was highly likely that their thoughts, which they prudently kept to themselves, were wide of the mark.

By nine o'clock that evening, we were lying on the bottom some two miles off the French coast. Dieppe lay some distance to the south, out of sight and to the north, according to the charts, lay the small town of Biville.

It was now time for the Commander to give all possible information to the rest of the crew. There had to be no slip-up when the time came to take off the two agents, and every man had to know his duties. That was imperative.

90

The wind had freshened a little and to make matters worse there was going to be a moon later on. In the narrowness of the torpedo compartment, the crew had been assembled and mustered. Only those on essential duties were absent and they would learn of our change of plans in a short while.

Hardly anyone spoke as the Commander entered and looked about him for a moment, before speaking. He came straight to the point, as usual:

" To-night," he began, " we're going as far inshore as we dare to pick up a couple of British agents who are being taken out of France and back to London. Apparently, we were the nearest submarine to the area and as the matter was urgent, we were directed to take these men off.

" I think I ought to mention at the outset that this is going to be more tricky than our usual operations. The enemy will have this stretch of the coast closely guarded. Probably there will be searchlights and once we're spotted, we will have to make a snap getaway. Is that quite clear ? "

There were low murmurs of assent.

" Good. Briefly, the position is this: precisely at eleven-thirty we will begin to move in, at maximum depth. I don't want to risk being seen.

" This mission is both difficult and dangerous. It is imperative that we get these men on board and head back to sea before the enemy troops have time to realise what is happening otherwise much valuable information will be lost."

He paused, glanced down at his watch. " There are two hours yet before we begin to move. All those who wish, can get a couple of hours sleep. I want every man on his toes as soon as we start for the shore."

The silence after the Commander's short speech was almost uncanny. For a long moment, no-one spoke. Then there came the usual shuffling of feet and the nervous coughing of men not quite at ease.

But it was also obvious that his talk had done something to relieve the tension which had been building up over the long hours of the morning and the afternoon. At least they now knew what they were to do.

It was impossible to sleep in the quietness of the ward-room. The utter silence seemed to get on my nerves and the sensation that we were heading into something un-known continued to build itself up inside my brain.

I found myself wondering where these two agents were at that moment. Running loose somewhere in the French countryside with half of the enemy troops after them. Was our lot any worse or dangerous than theirs ? Somehow I did not think so.

The time crept by with an insufferable slowness. I tried to fall asleep, but it was no good. At last it was 23.00 hours. The crew made their way slowly to action stations.

" Commander to crew. Prepare to surface ! "

Main vents checked and rechecked. We planed slowly to the surface as the electric motors hummed. A moment later, the periscope motor started up and the steel length of the seeing eye of the *Tamaranth* slid up out of its dark well.

The periscope broke water. Tensed, Richards took a quick, nervous look around. A moment later, he relaxed.

" Nothing there," he muttered. " Send her up ! "

We surfaced and clambered onto the bridge. Our speed had been reduced to less than three knots. There was scarcely a ripple at our wake as we slid through the warm darkness towards the distant coast.

Richards was gazing dubiously straight ahead. Now that we had our position taped, the only problem now was silence and alertness. Anywhere now we might run into trouble. A shore battery. Something wrong on shore.

I wondered what the Commander was thinking about at that moment. Certainly not about the ships we had passed up to get here unseen. That had all been in the luck of the game. This job in hand was of far greater importance.

Eyes were peering tensely in all directions. Shadows seemed to pop up all over the place, only to vanish mysteriously as we neared them. Richards cursed under his breath. The diesels were hammering faintly as they thrust the *Tamaranth* forward.

" See anything yet ? " asked Richards in a low voice.

" Nothing yet, sir." The same reply came back from both lookouts. So far, we were safe.

23.15 hours. The coast was a dark, irregular line, faintly visible. Overhead, the sky was quite clear, devoid of cloud, giving the navigator plenty of opportunity to check our position with a star sight whenever he needed one.

Every five minutes, the depth of the water around us was checked and later, as we approached the shore, this action was carried out every minute. There was no sense in running risks and beaching the submarine at the crucial moment.

The rocky nature of the coast was now clearly visible. We remained on the surface, watching tensely for the first sign of life among the darkness of the rocks. Every few

moments, Richards glanced down at the luminous dial of
the watch on his wrist, twisting his lips as the minutes slipped by and nothing showed.

" Where the devil can they have got to ? " he muttered
sharply. " They were supposed to be here two minutes
ago."

" Maybe something's gone wrong, sir." I peered
through the binoculars, allowing my gaze to move over
the full length of the visible coastline.

" God ! I hope not. We can't stay here all night,
waiting for them to turn up. The Jerries will have patrol
boats out around these waters. We might run into one
of them at any minute; and the longer we hang around,
the more chance there is that we'll be discovered."

" Perhaps if we were to— " I broke off at a sudden
whispered hiss from one of the lookouts.

" Light flashing off the port bow, sir."

Richards was alert in an instant. He swung round
slightly, bracing himself against the windbreak, his binoculars pressed against his face.

Even without the binoculars, it was possible to make out
the shaded flashing dots and dashes emanating from a
point low down in the lee of the rocks. Whoever it was
flashing the signal out to us, they had picked the best spot
under the circumstances. It would be impossible for it to
be picked out by anyone on the shore unless he happened
to be on the same level as the signaller.

One of the small dinghies was launched with two men in
it and slowly, it bobbed away into the darkness as the night
swallowed it up. Meanwhile, replying signals were being
flashed in carefully shaded dots and dashes.

Five minutes later, the flashing from the shore ceased

and we waited in silence. Had everything gone according to plan ? It was impossible to tell.

"God, but I'd sooner creep up on a cruiser than go through this again," muttered Richards as the seconds began to lengthen.

There were moments when it seemed as though everything around us was standing quite still, totally alien to sound. An entire world that trembled on the brink of an abyss of silence in which nothing moved. Then, quite, suddenly, there came the sudden sound of a shot, carrying across the water. It was followed almost immediately by another, and then by a fusilade of riflefire. A small searchlight sprang into being and began to sweep the water methodically.

"Hellfire. They've been spotted." Richards almost shouted the words. " Prepare to dive as soon as I give the word."

Slowly, the beam of the searchlight began to creep towards us, lighting the surface of the sea, leaving no room in which anything could hide.

"They've guessed there must be a submarine out here somewhere," I said.

"That means we'll have the entire coast batteries on top of us before we know where we are." Richards sounded anxious.

Barely a minute later, we heard the sound of oars splashing off the port bow and an instant afterwards, the sausage shape of the dinghy appeared, drawing rapidly closer. There were four men in it and one of them looked to be wounded. He sat huddled in the bottom of the dinghy, holding his right arm.

" Quickly ! Get them on board before the guards give a general alarm, if they haven't already done so."

One by one, the men were passed down the ladder to safety, the Commander and I following them. Last of all came the lookouts, piling down the narrow ladder as though all the devils of hell were on their heels.

The hatch slammed shut and was secured. Richards wasted no time. The order was given to flood the tanks and submerge. We lay doggo for half an hour before daring to move out to the open sea. At the end of that time, we slipped quietly westwards, away from the coast into deeper water.

01.20 hours and we ran into a group of enemy destroyers, obviously hunting for us. They knew we were there, somewhere and were determined to destroy us.

" Absolute silence," ordered Richards sharply.

The sound of the enemy destroyers' propellers was clearly audible now, threshing through the water above us. We waited tensely, every man casting fearful glances upwards, as though trying to pierce the steel and water above us, to see whether there were any depth charges on the way down.

After a little while they went away and the sound of them faded into the distance, but they returned twenty minutes later, just as we thought we had lost them. A group of explosions all around us, some uncomfortably close, told us that the depth charges had started falling.

" They're probably guessing," said Richards finally. " They're still not sure where we are. Otherwise, they'd be closer than that, believe me."

We had got into the coast all right and picked up our agents. Now, all that remained was to get them out in one piece. And from the look of things, that was not going to be as easy as it sounded.

"The information these agents are carrying must be pretty important if the Jerries want to make sure they don't get back with it alive," I said finally. "I've never known them go after a submarine with so much effort. They must be scattering depth charges around like confetti."

"Probably we've pricked their vanity," muttered Richards in reply. "They don't like to think that their defences are so lax that they can allow a British submarine to go in any time it likes and pick up two important men."

There was no further opportunity for reflections. Cautiously we edged ourselves out to sea. An hour later, the threshing of propellers faded into the distance and did not return. We planed slowly to the surface while Richards took a look around.

Nothing around. Still quite dark, but the moon was coming up in the east, its presence heralded by a silver glow brightening the horizon.

The wounded man had received bullet wounds in the right arm and shoulder, but after dressing them he seemed quite at ease. We learned later that they had been denounced to the Gestapo, but had managed to reach the appointed rendezvous ahead of their pursuers.

The small dinghy had been fired on as they were pulling away from the rocky shore, but only the one man had been hit.

By dawn, we were well away form the area and heading back towards Dover. There was little activity during the following day. We spotted several smaller enemy vessels, but left them severely alone. Some of them might have been disguised minelayers or submarine chasers. In any case, we could not afford to give ourselves away.

Even in these waters, the presence of enemy U-boats was an ever-present menace and we had bigger fish on board. Three times in succession, we were forced to dive as enemy planes droned out of the low clouds, forcing us down.

By nightfall however, we were approaching the English coast and the tension began to relax slightly. Seven days after setting out on patrol, we berthed at Dover and the two agents were tranferred ashore to complete their journey to London.

It was not until several months later, that we learned they had captured the plans of the German defences around Dieppe which were to come in quite useful some time later when the Canadians and British Commandos raided the town.

X

DOWN TO THE SEA

FOUR p.m. somewhere off the coast of northern France. The past twelve weeks had seen little operational work. Most of the time had been spent in home waters in the English Channel, sometimes venturing forth, lurking submerged for enemy shipping which never turned up.

It was noticed, whenever we had time to notice, during intervals between diving, that several neutrals were still making their way towards German ports.

The chill afternoon passed without incident. The wintry sun lowered itself through the thin haze which hung suspended over the sea, a red disc with only synthetic heat, which soon began to drop over the edge of the world.

" God ! You need the patience of a saint, Number One," said Richards, shading his eyes against the glare of the setting sun. " Especially with this job. Twelve bloody weeks and nothing sent to the bottom. I'm beginning to think that we'll never see action again."

" They seemed to think that we would be back in Blighty." I reminded him.

"They always do." There was a touch of bitterness in the other's voice. "I'm beginning to think there's a damned jinx on this patrol."

It was quite true. The exhilaration we had all felt on setting out, had rapidly deflated like a pricked balloon. The Channel seemed totally bare of enemy shipping. Even the sky had been devoid of German aircraft which, in itself, seemed unusual.

Day after day had passed in useless, futile search. Richards must have contemplated moving his area of search many times in defiance of his orders, but he kept his thoughts to himself.

Towards evening, however, our luck began to turn for the better. The haze started to clear slightly and visibility improved somewhat. A couple of grey shapes showed up indistinctly on the swaying horizon, just visible from the bridge. The port lookout spotted them immediately. His yell brought Richards alert in an instant.

Through the binoculars, it was just possible to make them out. First the masts showed, then the superstructure and finally, the entire ship itself.

"Destroyers," I found myself saying.

"You're right. And two of them. This may be something big." Richards drew in his breath in a sudden intake of air and bit his lower lip. "We'd better look into this. But we'll have to watch our step. Two of them is something of a handful."

He paused and looked throught his binoculars again. What he saw must have pleased him for he nodded sharply and yelled.

"Prepare to flood. Down to periscope depth."

The deck watch pounded down the ladder into the

control room. Swiftly, Richards and I clambered down and listened for the hatch to snap shut. There was a tense moment as the tanks flooded and there came the faint hiss of escaping air.

The submarine tilted sharply as we sought to gain depth in the shortest possible time. There was no time to waste. The enemy destroyers were heading in our general direction. At any moment, we could be spotted and attacked.

Sub-Lieutenant Kenniston stood waiting for us, steadying himself as the *Tamaranth* levelled out at periscope depth. A tall, straight-backed officer with a thin, angular face and piercing brown eyes. His features were stiff with respect.

" We'll have to hurry," said Richards quickly. " This is the answer to our prayers. If we can get these two, I'll be more than satisfied."

" When do we go in to attack, sir ? " asked Kenniston, his face tight.

" Don't be in too much of a hurry," warned the Commander thinly. " Remember. Those are destroyers out there—not cargo liners. We'll have to be damned careful from now on. They could sink us in minutes if they once picked up our scent.

" We can't go charging in there like a bull at a fence. And we can't afford to keep sticking the bloody periscope up every second. They may have planes out. This has got to be handled very carefully."

" Yes, sir."

The Sub-Lieutenant's face relaxed slightly in a responsive smile.

We moved in slowly to the attack, keeping well down, the periscope sliding up and down in its dark well. This was something in the nature of a culmination.   The climax.

Quite suddenly, I had another feeling. A peculiar tensing of the faculties which preceded another shot at the enemy.   Richards snapped orders at machine-gun speed.

There was absolute quiet in the control room. An immense silence settled over the *Tamaranth*. Only the gentle purr of the electric motors disturbed it as we moved in slowly, circling slightly to starboard to pick ourselves an advantageous attacking position.

" Hell, they both seem to be too jumpy for my liking," mused Richards reflectively, after glancing through the eyepiece of the periscope for a few seconds longer than usual.   " They're up to something, there's no doubt about that."   He turned to me.

" Here, Number One. Take a look, but don't be too damned long about it. I don't particularly like the look of this."

He stepped aside and motioned me towards the seeing eye of the *Tamaranth*.   A touch of the controls and the tiny periscope motor whirred, bringing the great, slender steel tube up with it, rising gently from the well.

I had my eye to it, long before it actually broke water and consequently, there was a sliding film of oily swell running over the objective lens making it difficult to pick out anything clearly for a long moment.   Then, quite suddenly almost as though the entire scene had been wiped clean by some magic erasing brush, details clarified.

The two German destroyers were clearly visible, less than a quarter of a mile away off the starboard bow, a white bow-wave bobbing around them as they thrust on through the heavy swell.

Their superstructure was clearly apparent and it was easy to see why Richards was uneasy. When first spotted, they had been pursuing a straight course. Now, they were weaving erratically from side to side, evidently searching for us. Had we been seen? Somehow, it did not seem likely, but then there was no way of telling with any degree of certainty.

After satisfying myself as to their present course and distance, I lowered the periscope and looked across at Richards.

" Well ? " he asked thinly. " What do you think, Number One ? "

" They're certainly acting strangely. Almost as though they knew we were here. But that's impossible."

" Is it ? " There was a trace of doubt in the other's deep voice. He shook his head dubiously. " We'll have to act on the assumption that we might have been seen when we were surfaced. We've been lucky so far in that they haven't got our exact position. Otherwise, the depth charges would be dropping by now."

The *Tamaranth* sliced her way through the heaving water, cold and dark and silent. Every watertight compartment in the ship had been closed up. The crew were at action stations. Torpedo tubes were all clear and ready for firing. This time, with a couple of enemy destroyers playing tag with us overhead, there might never be a second chance if anything went wrong.

Except for the steady beating of her electrical heart, turning the screws that drove her forward at a steady eight knots, there would be no indication of her presence to the watchful destroyers above.

" Any chance of it just being a routine operation up there,

sir ? " asked Kenniston, breaking the silence. " Those destroyers could be going through a routine practice battle and by coincidence they've chosen this area in which to carry it out."

" Could be," Richards nodded his head in agreement. He paused reflectively. " But the odds are stacked against it. He opened his mouth to add something more, but it was never said; because at that moment, the sound of propellers passing almost directly overhead suddenly made itself heard.

" Quiet ! " The Commander almost hissed the word. He spoke softly and urgently into the microphone. " Stop all motors ! Immediately ! "

The whirr of the electric motors ceased almost before he had finished speaking. Richards came upright over the microphone. His face was taut and the fine lines around the corners of his eyes and the edges of his mouth seemed to have tightened just a shade. But apart from that, he gave no outward sign of worry.

There was the peculiar sensation of drifting motionless in a dense void in which nothing seemed to move apart from the gentle back and forth motion of the submarine. If only we had been able to *see* what was going on up there. More than anything else, it was the feeling of not being able to do anything about the situation, not being able to move or make the first move.

With a startling suddenness, a disembodied voice called, urgently. " Destroyer propellers moving away, sir."

The tension began to relax a little. Taut muscles eased slightly from the positions which strain had forced them to take. Two men were standing with their heads held well back on their shoulders, peering intently at the steel hull of the *Tamaranth* above them, as though trying to pierce the thickness of metal and see what was happening above us.

The Commander waited until the sound of the threshing destroyers had faded into the distance before taking the periscope up again. The motors were still stopped. Cautiously, the metal snout of the periscope broke surface We were not left in any doubt as to the position of our quarry for long. Richards sucked in his breath, then said harshly.

" They're moving away and fast, but turning slightly. It may mean that they'll be coming back to execute another sweep pretty soon. The sooner we get into an attacking position, the easier I'll feel."

He turned and spoke into the microphone. " Start motors. Port ten. Full speed."

The electric motors started up again and the steady swaying motion of hanging unmoving in the water vanished and there was the normality of forward movement again.

" Keep your eye on them, Number one," said Richards quietly.

Through the periscope, the sea was only just visible now, fanged ridges of white foam and wind-tossed spray. It was difficult to make out the grey silhouettes of the destroyers against the darkening skyline, but they were there all right. There was no doubt about that.

A moment later, there were the two of them again, knifing round in a sharp, heeling turn that sent the spray tossing over their bows. It seemed almost unreal, watching them sliding gracefully through the troughs of the waves, bows splitting the water in a knife-edge of steel.

For a second, I had a paralysing thought: Had their first run merely been a feinting attack to judge our position and lull us into a false sense of security, in preparation for the final attack which was due to be delivered at any moment.?

But there had been no depth charges, and no destroyer Captain in his right mind would pass directly over an enemy submarine, knowing it was there, and not drop a pattern of depth charges behind him.

Meanwhile, everything on board the *Tamaranth* was going like clockwork. The crew stood by and waited in tense expectancy for the order to attack. This time, it was going to be a case of the man who got his punch in first. All we had to do was drive a torpedo through the steel hide of one of the destroyers to cripple it for the remainder of the action.

But the mere act of firing a torpedo, even if it struck home, meant that we would have to give away our position. The second destroyer would immediately bring all her guns and other resources to bear on us. But the chance to get a crack at these ships was one which was too good to pass up simply because risks would have to be taken.

It was an uncomfortable feeling to stand there, watching potential destruction racing towards us at twenty knots and know that everything, life and death perhaps, depended on the accuracy with which one torpedo was fired.

Richards took over a few moments later, screwing up his face in tense concentration. " Stand by tubes one and four," he ordered sharply.

" Tubes ready, sir." The answer was automatic. The Commander would not have expected anything else. He had trained this crew himself. The majority of them had been with him during the past year or so, knew his whims and mannerisms. At a time like this, there had to be no delay. Seconds were precious.

" Starboard three degrees."

The turning of the *Tamaranth* was barely perceptible. But it, too, must have been carried out without delay, for Richards nodded his head absently with satisfaction.

Seconds seemed like hours. Surely, I thought furiously, the destroyers should be within range by now. Why on Earth didn't the Commander give the order to fire the torpedoes ? I choked back my impatience. The Old Man would fire as soon as he was ready—and not before. And that would be when the sleek silhouette of the leading destroyer, scarcely visible against the darkness, crossed the intersection of the fine spider-wires.

Everything could be lost on that split second of time between getting the target exactly in the sights and loosing off the torpedoes too soon.

Behind the loaded torpedo tubes, the torpedomen would be waiting, ready, silent. Their bodies would be crouched with the urgency of the next move after the firing of the torpedoes and the cramped space in the torpedo compartment.

" Tubes one and four—fire ! "

I released my breath in a single exhalation of relief and felt, almost simultaneously, the shudder as compressed air sent death and destruction spearing through the water. The torpedoes had been sent on their way now. Everything was out of our hands. Nothing could stop them or turn them in the slightest once they had been fired.

Someone began to count the seconds laboriously.

Tension mounted a little. Richards, at the periscope, kept watch on the approaching destroyers. Had the torpedo track been spotted? If so, the ship concerned would undoubtedly be taking drastic avoiding action.

"Still proceeding on their original course," said the Commander finally. "They can't have spotted the track yet. By now, it must be too late if either of those tin fish were on the target."

We were not long left in doubt as to whether they had been fired on course or not. A tremendous explosion rocked the submarine, sending me staggering against the hull. Richards hung onto the periscope grimly. This part of the proceedings he was determined not to miss.

"A direct hit," he yelled jubilantly. "Amidships. I think we can forget about her."

He had barely finished speaking before the second torpedo struck with a shattering thud, strangely muffled by its passage through the water.

Richards turned from the periscope. "Now to get the hell out of this position before the sister ship locates us. And that won't take them long. They'll be out for our blood within minutes unless I miss my guess."

Through the periscope, it was possible to make out the silhouette of the sinking ship, limmed by the glow from the fire which had already taken hold amidships. A menacing cloud of dense black smoke obscured most of the smaller details, but judging by the list to starboard, it would only be a matter of time before she went down.

Even as I watched, the scene began to drift out of the field of view of the periscope. A faint red glow persisted to one side of the lens for several seconds, then that too faded as we turned rapidly and started forward into the protective darkness of the night.

Somewhere out there in the blackness, lay the other destroyer, thoroughly alert by now and intent on our destruction.

XI

Surface Attack !

THE next few minutes were a blast of utter violence. The *Tamaranth* jerked with the recoil of a detonation wave as a pattern of depth charges exploded in the near distance. For an instant, it seemed that she must surely break in two and careen out of control as though punched by a gigantic fist.

Then, miraculously, she steadied. No water ingress was reported from the various compartments and it seemed that, for the moment, we had escaped with minor damage.

All that I had ever learned was working through my brain with lightning speed as the threshing note of the destroyer's propellers became suddenly audible. We lay crouched some twenty feet below her, as silent as the grave, waiting for the second depth charge pattern to fall.

Already, in my mind's eye, I could visualise what was happening up there on the destroyer's deck. The clang of engine room telegraphs merging imperceptibly with the shrill clangour of the alarm. Submarine detected in the vicinity ! As if they didn't already know that with one of their ships sinking quickly by the stern with a couple of torpedoes in her.

I smiled inwardly. This was where their planning would have to come into play. A cat and mouse game. Tracking us across the sea, waiting to wreak vengeance on us for the surprise attack which had destroyed their sister ship. The white wake of the two torpedoes would have been noticed, especially the second, once the presence of a submarine was known.

They would have traced them back to their probable starting point and guessed that that was where we lay. They would know, also, that it would take us a few precious minutes to get under way on another course.

The destroyer would be shuddering with speed now, urged on by all the power of her engines, the screws churning the water into foam, the torpedomen standing tensed beside the depth-charge release levers, waiting for the order to send another diamond pattern hurling through the air, to land with a series of faint splashes in the sea astern.

From the throwers on the quarter-deck, the charges would spin high into the air under their propelling charge of cordite, turning over and over, before falling into the sea, dropping slowly until they reached their pre-determined depth.

Then, they would explode in a split second of unparalleled violence and if they were near enough, the outer hull of the lurking *Tamaranth* would split wide open like paper and the angry, furious sea would pour in, flooding and drowning. There would be little chance of escape.

There came another explosion, nearer this time. Then

again and again and again. Four. And we were still in
one piece as far as we could tell. It certainly didn't feel
any different after the depth charges had exploded. They
must have been quite a distance away.

Richards wiped his forehead. Beads of sweat stood out
on his face. " Hell. That was closer than I like to hear
those bloody things," he said tautly. " Just a little too
close, for my liking."

For twenty minutes, the *Tamaranth* swung and twisted,
seeking to throw off the vigilant search of the destroyer.
Several times, we thought we had thrown them off the
scent, only to hear the approach of propellers coming from
another direction.

Richards spoke quietly. " What's the tally ? Any
damage anywhere ? "

One by one, the reports came in. No serious damage
and no water coming in. Some minor damage, but that
was to be expected.

" It doesn't look as though we're going to throw them
off.   There's only one thing for it, if we're not to be sunk
by the next pattern of depth charges they throw at us.
We'll have to stop running and try to disable him sufficiently
with torpedoes. It may be possible then to attack him
with the surface gun."

He turned and must have seen the look of guarded surprise on my face, for he smiled thinly and said: " By the
look on your face, Number One, you don't agree with that
decision. I can quite understand that. On the face of it,
it would appear sheer suicide to engage the destroyer in a
gun duel, even if we do manage to disable him with a
torpedo.

" However, I assure you that it can be done, provided we act quickly and carefully."

I nodded. There was nothing for me to say. In the Navy, especially in the submarine service, trust in one's Commander is essential. The entire weight of the coming operation, which could mean either life or death to the entire crew, rested fairly and squarely on the Lieutenant-Commander's shoulders.

Such was the singleness of his authority. And this authority had been designated to him because of his skill in handling these craft and his previous experience in situations such as this.

If he said that we stood a chance in a gun duel with a disabled destroyer, then we stood a chance and that was all there was to it.

" Stand by torpedo tubes. Gun crew ready for action on surfacing ! "

Fighting it out with the 4.7 inchers of a destroyer was a bit chancy. Still, our own gun was a 4 incher although we possessed only one.

Tamaranth, its mighty tonnage of steel swinging slowly and easily under the thrust of the screws, trained itself on the distant target as the destroyer came racing towards us on its fourth sweep.

" They'll be too over-confident this time," said Richards thickly. " It might have helped if we'd blown some oil out through the empty torpedo tubes. Still, too late for that now, we'll have to make the best of things."

" You're relying on him thinking we must be pretty badly hit after those last attacks, sir ? " asked Kenniston.

" Something like that. At least, it should make him a little less cautious."

The control room fell silent as the Commander glued his eyes to the periscope. It would be difficult to make out the approaching destroyer now in the darkness, except for the white bow-wave flung up by her forward speed. But at least, they would have a still more difficult task to pick us out. Thank God there was no moon.

Richards spoke tensely as though his throat had gone suddenly dry.

" Numbers two and five tubes clear and ready."

" Tubes ready, sir."

Everything still going like clockwork. Nothing to do now but wait and hope that everything came off.

The gun crew were busily donning life-jackets and safety belts, with oilskins underneath. It was going to be bitterly cold outside, especially with the heavy swell lashing over the boat.

" Fire tubes ! "

An instant after he had given the order, the torpedoes were running towards their target. The first torpedo ran awry, missed the destroyer for some unknown reason. Perhaps it had been seen in time and avoiding action had been taken. If that were the case, the destroyer Captain had been damned quick off the mark.

The second torpedo however ran true to form. It struck the approaching destroyer in the bows, stopping her forward rush almost instantly.

" Fire tubes three and six ! " Richards' voice cut in on

my reverie. The *Tamaranth* jerked with the recoil as the torpedoes started on their journey. Two more thunderous explosions. Barely had the rumble died than the Commander was yelling orders at the top of his voice.

"Surface! Hurry! She won't stand there for ever waiting for us."

The control room seemed packed with men with scarcely any room in which to move. The gun crew, standing in a little knot by the base of the conning tower, were ready to go into immediate action. Each man knew the part he had to play and knew as well as the rest of us what we were up against.

Richards gave his orders as he kept the submarine trimmed. Scarcely had we broken surface than the gun crew were clattering up the ladder, out through the conning tower and racing across the slippery, wave-washed decks towards the gun. The destroyer was at a distance of almost half a mile, clearly visible in the darkness. There was no sign of the sister ship.

In all probability she had gone to the bottom during the hour that had elapsed since we had sent a couple of torpedoes into her. She had been in a sinking condition then, and it did not seem likely that we had travelled so great a distance that she had fallen below the level of the horizon and was still afloat.

"Open fire!" Richards snapped his order through clenched teeth. The wind was bitterly cold blowing from the south-east. There was no moon and the sky appeared to be overcast with an occasional star showing through breaks in the cloud.

The gun crew, crowded round the gun were swinging it

steadily, to bring its muzzle to bear on the distant target. And still there had been no firing from the destroyer.

" Funny they haven't opened fire on us so far," muttered Richards. " You'd have thought they would have a general idea of our position."

" Could be that they never expected us to surface. Only a fool would do that according to their way of thinking."

" Exactly," said Richards and there was a ring of amusement in his voice.

" Oh, I didn't mean it that way, sir," I protested volubly.

In the cold darkness, the Commander's muffled head shook slightly. " I realise that, Number One. But perhaps now you can see why we stand a chance. A slim one, I'll admit, but a chance all the same."

The four-incher opened up with a blasting bellow. There was no necessity for us to watch the reloading drill. That was exactly what these men had been trained for. They knew every wrinkle of the game, and when their very lives depended on it, one could rely on them not to make any stupid mistake.

The first shell must have fallen short of the distant target, for it was impossible to pick out any further explosion on board the destroyer. Fires had broken out and were raging furiously along the bow.

" She's pretty low down in the water, Number One," said Richards suddenly, breaking the uneasy silence. " Sho won't be able to make much headway with that load inside her, even if they do manage to start the engines. I think we're fairly safe now that she's a sitting duck."

" She still packs a punch though, sir," I pointed. There had been a brief orange flash from her guns a split second earlier while Richards had been speaking. It was followed almost immediately by the shrill whine of approaching shells. The salvo stuttered out of the air and struck the water less than fifty yards away.

The sea seemed to contract for a brief moment, then expand outwards in a great, billowing mushroom of water. Great gusts of wind blew the spray over the *Tamaranth*, drenching every man on the bridge.

Richards cursed volubly under his breath, but not once did he lower his binoculars. Those enemy shots had been too damned close to be healthy. It hadn't taken those b———ds on board the enemy destroyer long to get our range and position. They hadn't been too badly damaged.

In spite of the nearness of the enemy's shells, the gun on the foredeck of the *Tamaranth* was still blasting away, thundering its wrath at the distant enemy. Moving quickly now that we were on the surface and the full power of the diesels were thrusting us forward, we slipped nearer the stricken German destroyer.

Shells screeched into the night in rapid succession, heading in the direction of the enemy vessel. Through the binoculars, it was just possible to pick out the flashes of the shells as they struck their goal.

" Hold that direction and range," yelled Richards at the pitch of his voice. " You're on to her."

The *Tamaranth* was shuddering angrily at every shot of the gun as though surprised at her own temerity in shooting it out with something as big and heavily armed as a destroyer. At the jerk of each broadside, it seemed as though she must surely push herself clean out of the water.

Gradually, the deafening roar of the four-incher faded to a dull background noise as the ears refused to take it in any longer. The men worked like slaves, thrusting the shells home, taking aim and firing. There was no time for them to pause and cast a glance at the target to see what effect their shells were having.

But even as we were firing, the enemy destroyer was hitting back. Slugging it out with both fists. Shells crashed into the water less than twenty yards from us, as we turned to go in from the north. Gently, we slipped round, approaching from the starboard side of the destroyer.

All around us, the surface of the sea appeared to be convulsed by leaping pillars of foam that seemed to glow with a light all their own in the darkness. Scattered gleams of phosphorescence gave the entire scene a macabre glow.

There were long minutes of pregnant suspense, followed by further salvos screaming in both directions. How badly, the other was being hit, it was difficult to tell. The torpedoes which had struck home had gone a long way towards making her difficult to manage.

Whether her engines had been put out of commission completely, it was difficult to judge. But she did not seem to be making any headway at all against the running swell.

" I think she's just about finished," muttered Richards finally. He lowered his binoculars. " Better give her a couple more shots, just to make sure. I wouldn't like to think that she'll still remain afloat after all the trouble we've taken over this little job."

Two destroyers sunk by a single submarine. A feat almost unheard of. Only by sheer audacity had we been able to pull it off. The fates had definitely been on our side from the very beginning during this particular action. There was no doubt about that.

Had things swung the other way, as they could easily have done, we would have been sent hurtling to the bottom. Sheer, blind luck had taken a hand in the proceedings several times, and always it had worked for us.

A feeling of exultation ran through my veins. We drove forward through twin plumes of thrown-up spray as a couple of shells landed directly ahead of us.

" Cease firing."

The gun fell silent and a deep, uneasy calm dropped across the water. There came the distinct *boom* of the destroyer's guns and the thin screech of shells hurtling towards their target. Barely had they burst over on the starboard bow, than another, more prolonged, explosion rumbled across the distance separating us from the sinking destroyer. A shuddering, colossal detonation. Ahead of us, low down in the water, a giant flame roared up towards the heavens, shot through with a sullen, vivid glow that waxed and waned in a surprising manner.

A tall, spiralling mushroom of smoke, red at the base, climbed slowly and ponderously into the night sky. Fire raced and licked in fingers of burning oil across the surface of the water.

The bridge was suddenly stilled. For a long moment, nobody spoke. The gun-crew, dark figures, indistinct in their oilskins and life-belts, stood in a tiny, wondering group, looking out across the intervening distance.

" That's the finish of her," said Richards quietly, speaking in a low voice. " She's blown up. Those last shells must have hit one of the magazines. There won't be much left of her in ten minutes or so. Very few survivors."

His prophesy proved to be correct. At the end of five minutes we sailed cautiously towards the area of the explosion. Bits of wreckage tossed up and down on the oil-shot water, rising and falling over the crests and into the deep troughs.

Occasionally, something would slide past the side of the *Tamaranth* and vanish in the streaming wake. There would be a fragmentary glimpse of a dead, white face staring sightlessly at us before the sea snatched the body away, almost hungrily, and pulled it away out of sight.

" Well, that's the end of her," said the Commander slowly. He seemed to mull the words over in his mind before speaking them out loud. " Two less to worry about when the time comes for a final show-down. I can't say I'm sorry to see them go down."

" You're getting to be extremely bitter, sir," I said after a moment's reflective pause.

Richards nodded after an instant, " I suppose you're right at that," he said gently. " But war makes you vicious and bitter. It's something you can't help. I had a brother on one of the ships bringing the British troops back from Norway, when they were forced to pull out. He went down after being attacked by a Jerry destroyer.

" That's one of the reasons why I am always ready to send one to the bottom. Tonight, we've got rid of two of them. Maybe I am being a little unreasonable. But they had it coming to them. They wouldn't have hesitated to sink us if they had had the chance."

He ordered everybody down below, out of the night before charging the batteries. We were still too close to the enemy held coast to run on the surface for long periods with any degree of safety and half an hour later, we submerged and started off to look for fresh victims, every man refreshed by our moment of triumph.

XII

Air Attack !

THE sea was running high the next morning and the sky was overcast, thickly populated by clouds from which an enemy aircraft might pop at any moment. In the Officers' Mess, a hurried meal was eaten with the crockery sliding in all directions making it difficult to eat properly.

After the night before, we listened out on the radio, hoping to pick up a German news broadcast, announcing the sinking of two German destroyers by a flotilla of British submarines operating in the area immediately off the coast of France.

Although the radio operator managed to pick up several German radio stations broadcasting, there was no mention of the previous night's action, although several claims from from enemy U-Boats to have sunk many thousand tons of British and Allied shipping came through.

Richards merely shrugged when he heard the news. " They wouldn't dare broadcast it," he declared adamantly. " It would be as good as admitting a major defeat. Don't

worry, as long as their U-Boats are sinking our ships, they'll
never mention their reverses."

" Hell, but I'll bet they're mad at German Naval Intel-
ligence," muttered Kenniston. He glanced up from his
plate eyeing each of us in turn. There was an irrepressible
twinkle in his eye and a grin on his face. Nothing seemed
to get him down.

An hour later, we sighted the French coast some three
miles away, almost hidden behind a squall of rain. We
altered course accordingly and headed out to sea again.
From the navigator I gathered that the action of the night
before had introduced an uncertainty into his calculations,
and the impossibility of getting a star sight afterwards had
made it difficult to tell our position to within a couple of
miles.

Shortly before noon, with the sea still deserted of shipping,
I turned in. It was difficult to sleep. Even in the cool
darkness of the wardroom, the knowledge that outside,
some fifty feet above my head, it was broad daylight,
persisted in running through my mind.

I had never really been able to sleep properly during the
daytime. Sleeping at night, had become a habit with me,
and consequently, I had more than once, found myself at a
disadvantage compared with the other members of the crew,
who managed to snatch a couple of hours sleep at any time,
whenever the opportunity presented itself, and wake
refreshed, as though they had slept all night.

The submarine tilted lazily in the running swell. Somebody rattled crockery further along the corridor towards
the galley. The usual sound. So very different after the
spitting roar of the gun a few hours earlier.

It was unlikely that we should run into such big trouble

in the near future. Most probably it would be the usual round of empty seas and the constant watch for enemy aircraft. At any moment, the German Naval Command would order a renewal of the patrolling of the area in which we were operating. There would have to be some action taken after the destruction of two of their destroyers.

All these thoughts and a multitude of others were running through my mind as I lay there on the bunk and tried to fall asleep. The low murmur of conversation reached me through the bulkhead.

Listening to it, I fell asleep and woke three hours later to the shrill ringing of the alarm. The clatter of booted feet in the distance brought me fully awake. Something had been spotted, or we were under attack.

Pulling on my jacket, I headed in the direction of the control room. Richards was already there, his face wrinkled with concentration. I had time to take in the fact that we were diving, before Richards caught sight of me and motioned me forward with an urgent wave of his right hand.

" A couple of enemy aircraft hanging around up there," he muttered by way of explanation. "They came at us out of the clouds before we had time to get out of the way. No doubt about the fact that we were spotted. I'm expecting the bombs to start falling any— "

He broke off as the sound of objects splashing into the water almost directly overhead reached our ears distinctly. We waited tensely for them to explode. The seconds began to drag, stretching themselves out into individual eternities.

The control room was alive with men now, milling around in tiny, waiting groups. The first explosion thudded against the side of the *Tamaranth*. A split second later, the second came.

After that, there were no more. But what damage had been caused by those two explosions? At the time, it was impossible to guess. Confused shouting in the distance was sufficient to tell us that something had happened, that this time we had not got off with it so lightly.

Five minutes later, we knew the worst. One of the torpedo compartments aft had received most of the blast from the first bomb and water was pouring in through the ruptured hull. It would be necessary to surface.

Cursing his luck, Richards took the *Tamaranth* to the surface. It was difficult to handle the ship with water flooding into the rear compartment and no doubt, the knowledge that at least three men had been trapped in there, did not help his peace of mind.

We broke surface at an angle, but settled down almost immediately on a level keel.

" Gun crew up on deck," ordered the Commander tersely. " And I want the anti-aircraft guns manned too. Somehow, we've got to fight them off. It isn't going to be an easy job, but it's one that has to be done."

Men clambered hurriedly up the ladder and out through the conning tower, running to man the guns. On the bridge, Richards, scorning the heavy seas which occasionally slapped over the windbreak, watched them tensely.

" Hurry ! There isn't any time to waste. The second plane is heading in to drop his load on top of us ! "

Standing beside the Commander on the bridge, I debated whether to remain where I was, or to go below. It didn't help much to stand there and see what was coming, but at least there was the consolation of talking to somebody and knowing that if anything did go wrong, it would be possible to dive overboard, without being trapped below.

"Here he comes." Richards yelled the warning at the top of his voice, beating the port lookout to it by a split second. I swung my binoculars instinctively, searching the grey, leaden skies. There was too much cloud about to enable one to pick out a diving aircraft without difficulty.

A thin tremor of fear, momentarily dispelled by the action on the bridge, came back with a rush, surging through my brain. So this was it. Something far different from the attack of the previous night.

Then, the enemy destroyer, although a far more formidable menace than a couple of bombers, had been stationary, forced to a standstill by the detonation of the torpedoes. But enemy aircraft were a totally different matter. Utterly manoeuvrable, able to move with a vastly different magnitude of speed to ourselves, they represented a real menace.

"Open fire as soon as he comes within range," ordered Richards.

It seemed that the enemy bomber would pass almost directly overhead, but slightly ahead of the *Tamaranth*, something dropped from the belly of the plane. A couple of small black objects, dropping downwards with a steady motion, scarcely moving.

"Bombs dropping," called the port lookout.

Richards acknowledged the warning with a negligent lift of his free hand. A second later, the four-inch opened fire, spewing a stream of shells at the approaching plane.

The anti-aircraft guns aft of the bridge began firing almost immediately afterwards, sending tracer hurtling towards the Hienkel. It was impossible to see the effects of the tracer, but the bursting of the shells were easy to spot.

Black clouds of smoke puffing outwards, beautiful in their regularity, surrounding the twin-engined shape that rocketed overhead a second or two before the bombs exploded. An avalanch of ice-cold water rose high into the air, boiling outwards from the explosion in the centre. The *Tamaranth* spun helplessly for a moment, thrown off course by the explosion. The sea lifted itself into a mountain of dirty water, the blast screaming over the bridge, hurling salt spray into our faces.

Richards wiped his eyes with the back of his hand and put out his free hand to steady himself. The submarine steadied and ploughed on, still turning slightly to starboard to avoid the bombs.

The four-inch gun shifted to the second bomber already coming in on his second run. Behind us, the anti-aircraft guns were still trained on the first, passing away into the distance in a climbing turn.

Within seconds, however, he was out of range and they ceased firing reluctantly. The other bomber was still coming out of the steep turn which would bring him to bear directly on to us.

God, I thought furiously, why don't those gunners get those shells on the target for a change ? He looks big enough to hit.

There was a sudden moment of violence far too swift to be taken in fully. A puff of black smoke sprang into sudden being slightly below the oncoming bomber. The next instant, I had the momentary impression of a plane breaking up in mid-air, spiralling downwards with one wing ripped clean from the fuselage, as though sliced off by some invisible machete.

The bomber tilted out of the sky, a sudden burst of flame springing into life from the starboard engine. The bomber careered downwards, plunging straight for the sea.

It touched a moment later, trailing a white spume of spray behind it as it went under. Petrol brust into flames around it, enveloping it almost completely in smoke, making it difficult to pick out details. There was no sign of any of the crew.

"That's got one of the swine," muttered Kenniston through his teeth. "Now for the other."

"Nice bit of gunnery that," yelled Richards, scorning the use of the megaphone.

One of the gunners nodded, but there was no time for such congratulations, the second plane was already coming in on the last leg of his bombing run, determined to avenge the destruction of his companion.

XIII

The End of the Patrol

WATCHING the enemy bomber diving out of the cloud-driven sky, my throat tightened convulsively and there was the unpleasant sensation that the whole of my chest and stomach were forcing themselves up into my mouth.

Every pore of my face was oozing sweat as I pressed the binoculars into my eyes, staring through them at the black dot, rapidly growing into a definite shape.

This was it ! There was little hope in my mind that the gunners could repeat their victory over this plane as they had over the last. With direct action shell, it would have to be a direct hit to count. And the last shot which had sent the first Heinkel plunging into the sea, had been little more than a lucky fluke.

The gun jerked. Puffs of black smoke burst around the oncoming plane. Three black puffs with a faint flicker of red flame in the centre of each. They looked beautiful, but they weren't. A direct hit with one of those and a plane was a goner.

Richards stood rooted where he was, leaning forward

over the windbreak, casually yelling directions and ranges to the forward gun-crew. The anti-aircraft gunners would begin firing as soon as they could bring their guns to bear.

The bombs resolved themselves into black blobs streaking towards the *Tamaranth*, scarcely visible. It was impossible to tell where they would hit. An instant later, I lost sight of them as they approached the target.

" Get your head down Number One ! " Richards shouted the words at the top of his voice, ducking as he did so. His hand shot out, grabbed my wrist, and pulled me down behind the comparative shelter of the bridge.

The next moment, all hell seemed to have been let loose. The blast of the explosion almost lifted the submarine clean out of the water. She shivered, then steadied, ploughed on.

Close on the starboard side, the water gathered itself together, burst upwards with a shuddering of thunder and turned over at the top, showering us with spray. The second bomb dropped further astern, doing little damage.

Staggering, I pulled myself upright. The forward gun was still firing, but ceased reluctantly, when it could no longer bear on the bomber rocketing overhead. No sooner had it ceased its stentorian roar than there came the harsh chatter of the anti-aircraft guns taking over.

There was the acrid stench of burnt cordite blowing in the air, mingling with the salt of the spray. The Commander tried to pull himself to his feet, but failed and sank back onto the ridge.

There was a deep gash across his forehead from which the blood was running freely. He seemed only half conscious.

" You all right, sir ? " I forced my tone to be casual.

"Must have hit me somewhere in the leg. Can't move the damned thing. Give me a hand up, Number One."

I slipped my right arm under his and helped him to his feet. Hanging onto the windbreak, he managed to remain upright, his rugged features twisted into a grimace of pain.

"Hadn't you better go below, sir?" I asked. "He's bound to come in again. Probably with machine-guns this time."

"I'll go below when I'm good and ready, Lieutenant." Richards spoke sharply between thumps of pain. "And that won't be yet. Any other casualties?"

"Couldn't say at the moment, sir. I'll check on it."

I turned, but before I could shout across to the gunners, Richards stopped me. "Never mind about that now, Lieutenant, that blighter's coming round again. There's no time to be lost. You'd better take over for the moment, I think my leg's going to give out on me at any moment."

"Very good, sir."

The Commander steadied himself urgently against the bridge, trying to wipe the blood from his eyes with his free hand. He looked to be in pretty bad shape, but I knew better than to ask him to go below again, out of harm's way. He was a seaman through and through. Nothing short of death was going to drive him off the bridge.

He was impelled to remain there in the face of anything the enemy could throw against him, by an urge, an inner instinct which he could not have analysed even if there had been time for him to do so.

For ages, it seemed, the plane came round in a narrowing circle, banking steeply. The pilot meant business this time. The submarine had started to fire back at him on his first bombing run, had even dared to destroy his companion. Now, he intended to finish it for good.

A criss-cross of tracer burst from the Heinkel in flickers of fire and met that which poured up from the deck of the submarine. Richards, still leaning heavily on the bridge met the hail of bullets that spanged the steel. There was no time for him to duck down to safety with his injured leg.

Seeing it coming, I had thrown myself down instinctively. A second after the clattering of lead had ceased and with the sound of boosted engines still roaring in my ears, I felt something heavy fall on top of me, pinning my body to the ground.

For a moment, I lay on the cold steel of the bridge, unable to move. The inert body of the Commander cramped my movements in the limited space. It was only with the greatest difficulty that I managed to push myself up on my elbows and lever myself out from beneath him.

One glance was sufficient to tell me that he would not last long. There were at least five bullets in his chest, and it seemed impossible that at least one of them had not pierced his lungs.

I threw a swift glance around me for help. The forward gun turret was a shambles. Two men lay slumped on the smooth steel, moaning gently. The third was still standing by the gun, seemingly paralysed with fear.

There was no sign of either of the two forward lookouts. Either they had been killed outright by the fusillade of machine-gun bullets and been washed overboard into the sea, or they had been blown overboard by the blast of the bombs.

Whatever the cause, they were dead men by now and nothing could be done for them. The very idea of turning the *Tamaranth* to search for them in the hope of picking them up was ridiculous and the thought was immediately dismissed from my mind.

Richards' face was contorted with pain and blood from the gash over his right eye was running into it, so that it looked almost as though somebody had tipped a bottle of red ink over him. His mouth moved and jerked spamodically for several moments before any words came out.

Blood ran between his lips, oozing into his mouth. He reached up with his right hand, caught hold of my tunic, and pulled me down to him. There was an expression of single-minded concentration on his face which I had never noticed before.

" Take over command of the sub, Number One," he whispered hoarsely. " It looks as though you'll be taking over for good now. See if you can't take her back to Base. No sense in keeping her out here for the remainder of the mission in this state.

" She'll have to be patched up before she's really sea-worthy again. You understand all that, don't you, Number One ? "

I nodded. " Aye, aye, sir."

He seemed relieved at that and sank back, his head resting ludicrously against the upright of the windbreak. His eyes were half closed.

For a moment, I thought he was dead, his body seemed so still, his breathing so inaudible. Then, quite suddenly, he roused himself, and stared up at me, lifting his head with a terrible effort.

" That Heinkel, Number One ! Don't stand there looking at me. I'm nearly finished. Your first duty is to the *Tamaranth*. Never mind about me. That's an order."

" Very good, sir." I almost saluted by force of habit. Then remembered just in time. Throwing a quick glance at the cloudy sky, I saw that the plane was coming in again, for another run at us.

There was no time to get anyone else on deck to man the four-inch gun. And it was doubtful whether the gunner already there, staring down at the bloody mess of his companions, was in any fit shape to fire it, let alone aim it at a diving plane.

That only left the oerlikons. We would have to rely on them. I threw a swift, appraising glance behind me. The gunners were standing as though in a trance, staring across at the bridge, obviously wondering what had happened to the Commander.

" Stand by those guns," I roared. " What the hell are you lot staring at ? There's a plane coming in with every intention of shooting us out of the water. Jump to it ! "

The cold certainty of coming action seemed to clamp itself around my seething brain. Everything but the operation which was to come, seemed to be washed away, miraculously. My mind was ticking over like lightning.

Keep the submarine headed into the direction of approach of the aircraft. That was the only way to dodge most of what was coming.

With a shuddering roar, the Heinkel screamed down on us. Bullets hammered like peas off the bridge. Ducking instinctively, I half fell over the body of the Commander. He gave a low moan, then fell silent.

The oerlikons met the incoming plane with a hail of fire. A neat pattern of tracer streams sped upwards, beating into him, nailing him through, seeming to stitch him to the clouded sky with trails of fire and flame.

With a thundering bellow he was overhead, the last bullets from his guns spitting futilely into the water to our rear. With an effort, I forced my muscles to respond and obey my will. Clinging to the bridge, I refocussed my stultified vision on the scene around me.

The starboard oerlikon had ceased firing. The gunner lay in a twisted heap on the deck. The other gun was still blazing away at the receding bomber, now falling gracefully towards the water, trailing a black plume of smoke from one engine.

Pulling myself together, I remembered that for the moment I was in command of the *Tamaranth* and there was work to be done.

" First aid party on the bridge ! " I yelled. " At the double ! "

They came clattering up the ladder, swinging themselves onto the deck. Some paused to look down at the Commander, lying slumped against the metalwork, his eyes half closed.

" Get the Lieutenant-Commander down below," I ordered. " And be careful how you handle him. He's been pretty badly shot up. I'll see to some of the others."

The gunner manning the starboard oerlikon had been killed outright by the hail of bullets. There was nothing that could be done for him. The other gunner had been hit in the arm, but had managed to keep firing.

A minute later, the Heinkel, dipping swiftly towards the sea, hit the water, throwing up a vast cloud of foam-edged spray behind it. But there was no time to watch and see how soon it broke up under the force of the crash, nor whether there were any survivors.

A radio message would have been sent to the shore,

warning them of our presence and giving details of our position. Once those messages ceased to be transmitted, the mainland would know that something had gone wrong, and would send out surface craft to finish the job which the Heinkels had started.

The sooner we got out of that particular area and made ourselves scarce, the better. There were several wounded to be considered, including the Commander, and we would be forced to remain on the surface. Some material damage had been suffered during the bombing attacks, and it would be suicide to submerge.

The ingress of water in the rear torpedo compartment had been checked and the affected area sealed off, but there was always the possibility that other compartments would give under the pressure of water, where they had been weakened by the blast of the bombs.

Apart from all these considerations, we would be able to make better time on the surface. Submerged, we could only travel at a bare nine knots, whereas on the surface, the diesels would carry us along at almost twice that speed.

Turning, we headed north-west towards the English coast, still some fifty miles distant. We were far too close to enemy held territory to think of sending out a distress signal. That would have been inviting trouble, bringing down the whole of the available German forces on our necks.

Late that afternoon, with most of the injuries, casualties and damage established, it was possible to dispose of the dead. The Commander was drugged with a hypodermic, unconscious.

There was no telling how long he would remain alive. With the wounds he had sustained during the initial attack, it seemed miraculous that he had not died earlier. Most of the afternoon, I spent on the bridge, with two fresh lookouts posted. Now, more than ever, it was necessary to steer clear of any enemy shipping.

Twice during the long hours of the grey afternoon, it seemed as though fate was not content with playing tricks on us, but was determined to prevent us from reaching base at all costs.

When we had been in first-class trim, looking for prospective victims, the seas had been deserted, with nothing in sight. No smoke had shown on the bleak horizons, there had been no sound of approaching propellers which might indicate the presence of a richly-loaded cargo vessel, just itching to be sent to the bottom.

Luck had deserted us. Only the two enemy destroyers had shown up to prevent us going back from patrol empty-handed. And then we had been forced to fight it out. Now, pervertly, the sea-lanes around the French coast seemed to be teeming with enemy shipping.

Three times during the afternoon, we spotted black smoke on the horizon and once, the vessel passed within three quarters of a mile of us, where we lay, wallowing in the heavy swell, doing our best to look inconspicuous. A steamer of perhaps seven thousand tons, heavily-laden with cargo. Philosophically, we watched it proceed on its way, unable to attack.

Like most German vessels at that period of the war, it would most likely be armed and there would perhaps be an escort ship, lying somewhere just out of sight over the horizon, but within earshot of an urgent radio message: *Am being attacked by enemy submarine* ...

No, I decided, best not to take any unnecessary chances.

It grieved us all to see these rich prizes slipping by in the darkening afternoon, unmolested. But there was the Commander to be considered and the other wounded men. The sooner we got them back to base, the more chance they had of living.

The sea washed and gurgled over the bow and the breeze freshened towards evening, becoming bitterly cold. Kenniston, looking out across the scene of destruction forward of the bridge, said reflectively.

" Hell, but it must have been some fight. Pity I was below, I'd have liked to have been in it. Just think of it, two destroyers and a couple of Heinkels destroyed. God, but that's some record. Wait until the boys hear about this, back at Base. They'll never believe it."

" You should have seen the Old Man," I said quietly, nodding.

" Standing there as though he hadn't a care in the world. He even refused to leave the bridge after being wounded. God alone knows how he managed to stand the pain."

" He's one of the old school," said Kenniston thoughtfully.

" No bloody German is going to drive him off his bridge. He must have had plenty of guts to meet that hail, standing upright. And he must have known that the second time that blighter came in, he wouldn't stand much of a chance in ducking in time."

" Most likely he didn't know what fear was."

" Maybe." I said and fell silent. It was quiet now, with the grey dusk falling over the sea and the clouds gathering overhead. The time for the routine manning of the action positions. It was as though the entire surface of the sea was standing still. Afraid to move.

A quiet, grey eternity in which only the *Tamaranth* moved, surging forward relentlessly, thrusting aside the water with her bow, throwing it up as a knife-edged bow-wave that splashed away on either side of her streamlined shape.

Perhaps, I thought, the Commander had really been one of those few men who knew no fear, but somehow, I didn't think that had been the real reason behind his actions. Oh, yes, he knew what fear was all right. Everybody does.

The instinct of self-preservation is something which grows within us from the very first time, when as a child, we are suddenly confronted with loneliness and the dark. He knew how to keep his head and his mouth shut when ever death stared him in the face, defying it with all his will-power, never letting it get the better of him.

He declined to allow it to rule his thoughts and actions. He was Commander of a submarine and as such, he had had to show an example to the men. No doubt, it had not been easy. Such things never are. But if he had once given way to the elemental fear that strives to take over the mind, the men would have been quick to follow suit.

Only his superb example had kept them going. He could have given the command to me at any time after he had been wounded. Gone below, out of the way of the flying bullets, confident in the knowledge that he had fulfilled his duty to the letter.

But he was determined to do more, to go beyond all he need to do to satisfy his conscience. Going below and relinquishing his command in the middle of a battle, would have seemed like running away to his way of thinking.

No, he preferred to remain where he was and see it through to the bitter end. And now, he lay gravely wounded below, lying on his bunk in a drugged stupor.

XIV

Fresh Command

THREE days later, we limped into port and Richards was taken ashore. He was still alive, but how he had managed to hold on for so long, nobody seemed to know. One of the other wounded men had died barely sixteen hours before we had made port. In all, our casualties had been seven killed and twelve wounded.

After that, it was almost three months before the *Tamaranth* was ready for sea again. The damage had been far more serious and extensive than anticipated. I had not been present when they had brought the three bodies out from the flooded torpedo compartment at the rear of the submarine. It had not been a pleasant sight, I had been assured.

Richards was still in shore hospital, critically ill. Three of the others, less badly wounded, had been discharged but would not be accompanying us on this particular trip.

Most of all, we were looking forward to meeting the new Commander. So far, nobody seemed to know anything about him, nor even who he would be. The reason for the secrecy? Chiefly because of the usual red tape which attended such things in the Navy.

When the long-awaited message did arrive, however, it was a complete surprise. The signal arrived at ten o'clock on a grey January morning. Masson, climbed the bridge with it and handed it to me. I could see that it would be something of a surprise from the expression on his face.

Carefully, I opened it and read the contents. It was brief and to the point. I had been appointed temporarily in command. For the first time, I now had a command of my own. And it was the *Tamaranth*. Sometimes, one is unlucky in a way. An appointment to command, when it does come, normally means being drafted away from one's old ship, from the shipmates one has grown to know and become used to.

It was only infrequently, that something such as this happened. I thought of Lieutenant-Commander Richards and wondered how he had felt when he had first been appointed to command the *Tamaranth*. Probably much the same as I felt myself at that very moment.

It was something I would remember as long as I lived. I nodded to Masson. " Very good, Masson. See to it that the crew are ready for duty. I expect this means we'll be slipping out soon. Better make sure that everything is ready."

" Aye, aye, sir."

That very afternoon, the new Number One came on board. A tall, rangy Lieutenant, young but competent. He held himself with that indefinable air of complete command and knowledge of authority that normally went with a submarine Number One.

He seemed easy to talk to, on the surface, but underneath, I could sense the steel which picked out a good man from one who, although not bad, was indifferent. He seemed a nice bloke, one to whom the men would take. He would stand no nonsense, I decided as he went below, neither would he be unjust.

His name, it appeared, was Reynolds. This was his second submarine.

That evening, our sailing orders came through. We were returning to our first hunting ground, the coast of Norway and Denmark. Inwardly, I hoped that our luck would be better than on the last mission. Then, we had stretched our luck to its limit.

I had only time for a brief glimpse at the harbour and what it held. Several of the " T " class submarines were already berthed there, waiting their sailing orders. Some were in dry dock undergoing repairs. One, some distance away, appeared to have been blown almost in half. How she had managed to make base, was incredible. We learned later, that almost half of her crew had been killed when they ran foul of a German cruiser.

The slip-wire stretched itself into a bar of solid steel, taut and strained to the bull-ring. A hammer swung and it dropped lifelessly to the fore-deck. It was run in swiftly and we were heading out across the grey waters of the harbour.

Reynolds came up onto the bridge as we slipped our moorings and stood looking out over the harbour in silence for several minutes. There was a far-away look in his grey eyes. Almost as though his mind were a thousand miles away, in some world all its own.

" Not an ideal night for going out, sir," he said suddenly, turning his head.

" Maybe not, Lieutenant. But at least it'll keep the Jerry planes grounded. That's what happened to us last time."

Reynolds nodded his head slowly. " Yes, sir. I heard about it. Seems as though you struck it pretty rough from what I've been told. How's Lieutenant-Commander Richards getting on ? "

" Not too badly. He seems to be out of danger, but it's doubtful whether he'll see active service again. Not for a couple of years, anyway. And by that time, the war might be finished, one way or the other."

" Do you really think so, sir ? I mean about the war being finished."

" I don't know. It'll be a hell of a job getting men and material ashore on the continent. Even if we have the help of the French Resistance, the casualties will be heavy."

" What about the Russians ? Think they'll advance into Germany ? "

" Maybe. They have the men, but what about the arms ? You know as well as I do, that we're losing more men and ships than we can really afford on these Russian convoys. How long can we keep that up without damaging our own war effort ? "

" I'm beginning to see what you mean, sir. It does begin to look pretty hopeless, doesn't it ? "

" Not really. Hitler hasn't dared to risk an invasion of England and with the men and material which might come from America, I think we'll win through in the end, but it's unlikely to be as soon as some people seem to think. We mustn't underestimate the enemy, whatever we do."

Three days later, we were off the north Danish coast. A heavy sea was running, and for most of the time we ran submerged. It was safer that way and more comfortable. The swaying, bucking motion of the submarine was minimised to a very great extent, the deeper we went.

All night, nervously alert, we ploughed our way steadily north-east, keeping watch for enemy surface craft and aircraft. Over the past two weeks, reports had been received about enemy convoys running along the coast of Norway, hugging the shore, content in the knowledge that they were safe from our surface vessels and well away from the range of British bombers.

Submarines were another matter however, and it was probably for this reason, that the enemy had decided on the convoy system, working on the assumption that a British submarine would be loth to attack a convoy, especially if several of the ships were armed, whereas a single vessel would be readily attacked.

On the fourth morning, we sighted the tip of Denmark over on the starboard bow, a grey line seen through the mist, barely visible except through the binoculars. Throughout the entire trip, the *Tamaranth* had behaved perfectly. It was impossible to find any fault with her. The repairs seemed to be holding satisfactorily. The crew were in high spirits and confident, convinced that this time, we would be lucky.

With the final glimmer of a grey dawn giving way to a wintry redness as the sun, cold and without heat lifted itself above the eastern horizon, the Danish coast dropped away behind us and we turned towards our allotted area.

Whether the reports on convoys moving southwards

along the Norwegian coast were true or not, we were determined to find out for ourselves. I shook Reynolds, where he lay, dozing uneasily, with his back against the windbreak.

" Eh, Whassat ? " He struggled to his feet and stood swaying for a moment, peering about him.

" Time for your watch, Number One," I said quietly. " Better keep your eyes open, we're well into enemy waters now."

" Aye, aye, sir." He blinked his eyes and screwed them up against the glow of the sun.

I went below, to the wardroom. It seemed strange, that, after all the time I had sailed with Richards, I was now occupying his bunk.

Taking off my tunic, I lay down on the bunk and closed my eyes. It was the first time for almost two days that I had had a chance to snatch more than an hour's sleep at any one time. Even now, there was no guarantee that I would be allowed to sleep longer than an hour or so.

Reynolds had his orders to wake me the moment anything out of the ordinary appeared. And such an event could happen at any moment in this area.

Nothing did happen however, and it was almost four hours later when I was wakened by Kenniston, shaking me by the shoulder.

" Almost mid-day, sir," he said by way of greeting. " Nothing in sight yet, I'm afraid. Number One thinks there might be a storm blowing up. It's getting hellishly cold outside."

" That's only to be expected this time of year," I said, swinging my legs to the floor and groping for my tunic. " The Number One ought to know what he's talking about.

We'd better go up top and take a look. A storm could make it pretty bad for us. Reducing visibility to nothing."

"Yes, sir." Kenniston agreed in an undertone. Together we made our way up the conning tower, and squeezed our bodies out onto the bridge. Reynolds looked down to greet us.

"Nothing been sighted so far, Commander," he said quietly, efficiently. "The visibility is dropping alarmingly. Less than a quarter of a mile already and the wind seems to be blowing up for a gale."

He was right on that score at least, I thought, taking a quick look around. The white-topped waves were rising higher now, foaming over the bow and sending great clouds of spray over the bridge, soaking us to the skin.

"Very well, Number One. I'll take over now. You can go below. I'll let you know if anything happens. Frankly I doubt it. There can't be many ships out in weather like this. Most of them would make for the shelter of the coast. And unfortunately, we can't venture in that far."

"No, sir." Reynolds nodded and vanished below. The sound of his booted heels on the narrow ladder gradually faded away into silence and finally stopped altogether.

By one o'clock the wind had risen considerably. It was soon blowing with gale force and we experienced nothing but tremendous seas and mountainous waves that came lashing over the bridge, drenching us even through the protective oilskins. The weather worsened as the afternoon wore on. Visibility dropped still further, until it was impossible to see anything beyond a distance of twenty-five yards.

The barometer plunged to the depths, holding out little

hope of an improvement, at least in the very near future. The lookouts wore their life-belts, clinging onto their posts for dear life as sweeping seas threatened to sweep them overboard.

Huge waves came charging in at us from the weatherside, their motion exaggerated by their ponderous nature. Nothing, it seemed, could stand in their path, and still survive.

The evening came and went, deepening into night. One of the darkest nights we had ever known. Not a single star showed through the driving clouds and it was impossible to take a check on our position by means of a star-sight. For all we knew, we could have been blown off our course by several degrees.

The storm abated somewhat during the early hours of the morning, however, and we dived to check all installations. Running submerged was pleasant and quiet after the fury of the storm raging above us. It was while we were running submerged that the hydrophone operator picked up the noise of distant ships, a quiet singing that was unmistakable.

Slowly, we planed up to periscope depth, but it was impossible to see anything and there was little hope of making a check on their direction. After a careful periscope inspection of the entire area, I decided to head towards the coast as this would be the most likely place for an enemy vessel to be.

My hunch was eventually proved to be correct. As we approached the coast, still hidden in the darkness and the drizzling rain, the sound of propellers on the hydrophone grew distinctly louder.

"Sounds like something big, sir," said Kenniston, after a preliminary examination.

"I agree. But it's a pity we can't see him. In this damned rain, he could slip past us within ten thousand feet or so, and we wouldn't see him. God, if only this weather would clear and give us a chance to see."

We were still no wiser as to the course which the hidden enemy vessel was steering. It lay somewhere to the east of us as far as we were able to determine, but apart from that we knew nothing.

"There's nothing for it," I said finally. "We'll have to steer blind and hope that we come within striking distance before he spots us. Could be a decoy, a destroyer, on the lookout for submarines like us."

We surfaced five minutes later, and headed due east into the mist and the rain. There was a faint glimmer of light showing in the distance where the dawn was about to break. But apart from that, nothing broke the monotony of grey seas and the uneasy darkness which lay like a blanket over the furrowed ocean.

The minutes ticked by. Still no sign of her, although the hydrophone operator reported heavy signals coming in, getting stronger every second.

"She can't be far away," I muttered finally, screwing up my eyes behind the binoculars. If only the damned mist would clear !

"If we're not careful we'll run right into her, whoever she is," replied Reynolds, standing by my side, a grey, mist-wreathed figure, muffled up against the chill wind.

We looked at each other in bewildered wonderment. We were closing in at speed. Soon, if we did not spot her, we would be forced to change course, or slow engines.

She was getting just a little too close for comfort.

Fruitlessly, I searched the horizon, bounded by the rain and mist. Still nothing visible. Then, quite suddenly, without warning, the huge bulk of a ship loomed up out of the grey dimness, almost on top of us.

I had barely time to yell before Reynolds was shouting too: " Hard to starboard. Emergency. Diving stations. Flood."

The words tumbled from my lips in a blur of sound. How anyone managed to make sense out of them, I never knew. But somehow, they did.

The alarm bell rang raucously through the entire length and breadth of the *Tamaranth*. The lookouts clattered down the swaying ladder, jumping clear at the bottom, and Reynolds and I landed among them.

Above our heads, the hatch clanged fast. There was the sound of air being forced out of the tanks, to allow the ingress of water. Then we were going down, fast but not fast enough.

" Up periscope ! " The periscope engine whirred quietly and drew the slim length of the periscope up out of its well. The ship was dangerously close now, filling the entire field of vision. God, I thought, would the *Tamaranth* never begin her turn ? Had they mistaken my order ? A thousand possible complications surged through my seething brain and were ended, abruptly, conclusively, as the image of the ship began to slide across the cross-wires. We were turning.

But was the turn sharp enough ? Would we have time to spare ? It seemed doubtful. God ! Hurry. That ship won't take long in crushing us to pulp once she hits.

Breathlessly, I watched the vast bulk of the vessel moving towards us. We must have slid across the stern with scant inches to spare. I found myself wondering in a peculiar detached sort of way, whether anyone on board knew how close they had been to a British submarine.

There was no indication from the enemy vessel that they had guessed at our presence. Our electric engines were still running at full power and their hydrophones should have picked up the sound of them from that distance.

But once again, our luck held. Fate seemed to have come over onto our side for a change. Slowly, we withdrew to starboard of our victim, keeping her in sight, never once allowing her to slip away into the mist.

At two thousand yards, we released the first two torpedoes. There was no possibility of a miss in our minds and yet the first torpedo went astray. A miss.

What had happened nobody would ever know. Torpedoes were like that. Each had its individual idiosyncrasies, each its own destiny. If it were destined to score a direct hit, it would do so, no matter how wide of the target you appeared to have aimed it.

The second tin fish struck the vessel amidships, sending up a vast mushroom of grey smoke and flame. It was wonderful to watch the actions of the crew immediately after the burst of the torpedo.

Shaded lights began to flicker on board. Boats were lowered and the radio operator reported that no sooner had the explosion occurred, than the ship's radio operator had begun sending out warning and distress signals.

"I think it's time we got out of here—and fast," I muttered, turning away from the periscope. The enemy ship was listing heavily to starboard and it was obviously only a matter of time before she went to the bottom, together with her precious cargo.

The enemy radio operator was still sending out his frantic radio signals as we turned into the open sea. The stricken vessel was sufficiently near the coast for help to arrive for the survivors and none of them should be in the water for longer than an hour at the most.

But that also meant that we were in danger of being attacked by land-based aircraft, determined to wreak vengeance on us for the audacious sinking of the ship.

We raced away into the protective blackness. The clouds were beginning to break slightly overhead and it boded well to being a fine day.

Shortly after dawn, the weather cleared like magic and we remained on the surface, recharging the batteries and allowing fresh air to blow through the ship. Remaining underwater went a long way towards fouling the atmosphere below. It needed a regular spring-clean like this to make things bearable.

That afternoon, we spotted two more vessels steaming a south-westerly course. We approached cautiously. This could be a trap, although it did not look like one on the surface. However there was no point in taking any unnecessary chances, especially as far as the submarine itself was concerned.

The ships turned out to be medium-sized cargo vessels of about six thousand tons each. They were evidently carrying a very heavy cargo, possibly Norwegian iron-ore to feed the furnaces of the Third Reich.

Gently I brought the boat into position for an attack. There was no sign that they knew we were there and the torpedo attack was carried out like clockwork. The *Tamaranth* shook slightly. The torpedoes were running.

I had deliberately chosen the furthermost ship as the first target. There was nothing in the distance really, but it would give the impression to the nearer ship that the attack had come from the other quarter, with the result that she would most probably steer in our direction, towards the danger, rather than away from it.

This had been one of Lieutenant-Commander Richards' favourite tricks when hunting down two ships and it was one which always seemed to pay off dividends. I had never forgotten it.

Once again, it worked. There came the roar of the first explosions, echoing across the water. Almost immediately we saw the stuttering of shaded lights flashing between the ships, followed by a change of course on the part of the ship nearer to us.

" She's turning this way, sir," muttered Reynolds. " Is that what you expected ? "

" Exactly," I nodded. " Richards always used to pull that trick on them. I've never known it to fail yet. I turned to the microphone.

" Tubes Three and Six ready to fire ! "

" Tubes ready, sir."

I watched the slender shape of the enemy ship gliding gracefully across the circle of light of the periscope. Gradually the distance between it and the intersection of the crosswires closed. The intersection vanished against the vessel almost amidships.

" Fire tubes ! " I ordered.

It was impossible to make out the narrow tracks of white water traced out by the speeding torpedoes, but it was soon clear that they had been spotted by the lookouts on the enemy vessel. She began to alter course, rapidly, zig-zagging, striving to line herself up parallel to the on-coming torpedoes. Tensely, I found myself counting off the seconds. A minute passed. Had I misjudged the distance ? It did not seem likely, but it was something to be taken into account.

My thoughts were broken with a startling suddenness as a cavernous roar shattered the expectant silence and a vast pillar of fire lifted itself from the doomed vessel. A split second later, another erupted into a heaving of smoke and violence.

Two hits ! A writhing pall of flame-shot smoke was boiling up into the clouded sky. Then it spread out, mingled with that from the other ship and climbed higher and higher until it was indistinguishable from the clouds.

XV

The Price is Paid

For a further eight days we cruised through Norwegian waters without spotting any further enemy ships. It was beginning to look as though we had frightened them all away, driven them into harbour, where they were comparatively safe.

The wind had moderated considerably and backed to the south-east. Our fuel reserves were falling dangerously low and it would soon be time to think of heading for home.

On the evening of the tenth day after the sinking of the two enemy ships, I decided to continue the search for another twenty-four hours and if nothing showed up in that time, to turn and head for home.

Reynolds wanted to stay out longer in the hope of picking something up. So far, we had seen nothing of the convoys about which we had heard so much at Base. They had to be somewhere around, he argued.

His logic was unassailable, but there still remained the fact that we had seen nothing of them although we had scoured the entire area in which they were known to be operating. Either the information we had been given was wrong, or the enemy had grown wise to the fact that we knew of his plans and had altered them accordingly.

Whatever the reason, we spotted nothing on the following day and, reluctantly, we turned for home. There was no point in hanging around any longer in the hope of catching up with a convoy which might never turn up. And there would be hell to pay if we ran out of fuel before reaching base and had to be towed in.

The sky cleared remarkably on the way back, making it doubly difficult to spot aircraft. Against the brilliant background, they did not show up at all clearly.

Perhaps that was the reason why the enemy Heinkel was not spotted earlier. Our position was just south of the Orkneys when the first bombs began to fall. The knowledge that any enemy aircraft were able to operate in that vicinity, came as a distinctly unpleasant shock to me.

Standing on the bridge, there had been nothing in view the previous minute. The next, a vicious twin-engined shape had hurled itself over the *Tamaranth* before screaming away into the distance.

There was a sudden thunderous explosion as the two bombs dropped into the sea some fifty yards astern of the submarine, lifting twin gouts of water high into the air, before they fell back in a creaming of foam. The underwater detonation wave hammered against the plates of the stern, shaking the *Tamaranth* like a leaf in a gale.

" Hell! " swore Reynolds, turning his head swiftly and peering through his binoculars at the disappearing shape, now climbing steeply into the heavens.

" He'll be back again in a few minutes," I yelled. " Our best chance is to dive and get down as far as possible."

Within seconds, we were down below and the tanks were flooding with water. Swiftly we planed down to periscope depth, then continued to drop. The lower we went, the more chance there was of escaping serious damage.

But a compromise had to be made. If we were at too great a depth, the risk of damage was reduced, but if it did happen, we were finished. The submarine would plunge to the bottom like a stone. If we did not go down far enough, the enemy's bombs would not only damage us, but blow us to the surface, where we would be literally at his mercy.

A moment later, there came a roar that hurt my ears, beating against the ear-drums like the smack of a fist. The *Tamaranth* careened like a frightened beast and threatened to topple over on her side. For an instant, everything was topsy-turvy. The floor seemed to lurch up beneath my feet, making it impossible to stand upright.

From somewhere in the distance came the screaming of injured men and the dull roaring of water, surging into the ship.

Desperately, I staggered to my feet, clinging onto the nearby bulkhead for support. Kenniston and Reynolds were already pulling themselves upright. Fear and astonishment showed on their faces.

The *Tamaranth* appeared to be out of control. She would not answer her helm and appeared to be sinking slowly, although she was not plunging downward out of control as I had feared in that first brief moment of violence.

" Those bombs must have breached the hull." Kenniston was shouting the words at the top of his voice. I lurched

forward. As was normal practice, all bulkhead doors had
been closed for action stations. Our only contact now
with the men in the other compartments was by means of
the intercommunication system. Desperately, I called
compartment after compartment. In some of them, I
received a reply which said that they were still all right and
no water was coming in, but what the hell was happening
with the submarine ? Were we sinking—and what were
my orders.

After a complete survey of the ship by this method, the
overall picture clarified a little. The bombs had blown a
great hole in the hull of the submarine forward of the
torpedo compartment in the bows.

As far as I could make out, water had poured into the
compartment, drowning all the men already there. The
watertight door in the bulkhead, sealing that compartment
off from the torpedo storage room was holding so far, but
was not expected to hold for long. It too, it appeared,
had been damaged and weakened by the bomb blast.

The weight of water in the forward torpedo compartment
was the reason for the downward motion of the *Tamaranth*.
The electric motors too, seemed to have been put out of
action and we were helpless.

" Can we possibly surface, sir ? " asked Kenniston
anxiously.

" Frankly," I confessed, " I doubt it. There's nothing
for it but to abandon ship. Through the Davis escape
hatch. Quickly ! There's always a chance that the others
might be able to get out through the torpedo reloading
hatch, it's well aft of the area of damage. I'll give the
necessary orders."

After giving the order to abandon the *Tamaranth*, I found

myself a life jacket and strapped it around me. This was the first time I had been forced to use the Davis escape hatch under operational conditions. I had used it several times during practice tests, but never under conditions such as this.

Quickly, I made my way aft towards the compartments which housed the diesels and the electric motors. There was an uncanny silence over everything. When I arrived, Kenniston had already made his way through the hatch and Reynolds was preparing to follow.

"Any of the others escaped?" I asked.

He nodded. "Several of them had made their way here when she started to go down," he explained hurriedly. "I don't think there can be many left behind still in a condition to get out, sir."

The *Tamaranth* gave another lurch. That settled it. I followed Reynolds. The coldness of the water closed about me, making it difficult to hold my breath. There was the surging, upwards rush, the bubbling of water about me and then, seconds later, I broke surface, spluttering.

There were several of the crew already in the water, swimming around in circles. With an effort, I picked out the face of the radio operator, bobbing up and down in the water. I swam over to him.

"Did you have time to send out a distress signal?" I gasped.

He nodded. "I sent it out as soon as the bombs fell, sir." He spluttered as water went down into his mouth.

That, at least, was something hopeful. The message would have been picked up, there was no doubt in my mind about that. But how long before rescue arrived on the scene? The water was bitterly cold. It would not

take long for a man to die of exposure in this, I thought.
Savagely, I thrust the idea from my mind.

The Heinkel was still droning around, circling the area.
I wondered whether his radio signals had been picked up
too and would serve, inadvertently, to facilitate our rescue.

Half an hour passed and there was a chill numbness
spreading up my legs and into my body. My teeth were
chattering in my head. One of the telegraphists, some
distance away, suddenly went under. Someone swam
towards the spot, but he did not come up and we could only
guess that he had been too numbed to even put up a fight
for life.

At last, when it seemed that there would be no rescue,
the sound of engines reached our ears. At first, it was so
distant and far-away as to be almost inaudible. It seemed
to fade into silence at irregular intervals, but I soon realised
that this was brought about by the water slapping against
my ears, making it impossible to hear for seconds at a
time.

The engines turned out to belong to a fishing vessel
which appeared suddenly out of the thin mist, heading
directly towards us. Reynolds attempted to raise his hand
and wave, but he seemed too numbed to do anything.

Luckily, we were spotted and within minutes the fishing
vessel was alongside, hauling us on board. The Skipper,
a gruff Scot, with a broad accent, informed us that they had
picked up our distress signal and hurried to the scene as
soon as the approximate position had been given.

They had also been guided to us by the Heinkel, which
they had inadvertently mistaken for a Beaufighter, circling
us until help arrived. We never found out the name of

that Heinkel pilot who sank us and yet, in turn, saved our lives.

Twenty minutes later, we were heading back to the mainland. Out of the crew of fifty-three, we had lost twenty-six either killed, drowned or trapped in the *Tamaranth* when she went to the bottom.

As a submarine, she had been one of the best; and that was as good an epitaph as any to give her.

THE END